ANNE GREENE

A WILLIAMSBURG CHRISTMAS
BY
ANNE GREENE

Copyright Anne Greene 2018
Forget Me Not Romances, a division of Winged Publications

All rights reserved. No part of this publication may be reproduced, stored in a retrieval system, or transmitted in any form or by any means, with the exception of brief quotations in printed reviews.

This book is a work of fiction. The characters in this story are the product of the author's imagination and are completely fictitious.

All rights reserved.

ISBN-13: 979-8-3492-1752-4

DEDICATION

To my wonderful husband, Larry. Thank you for our love story.

Thank you for supporting me in this great adventure of being

an author. You are a gift from heaven. To my editor,

Cynthia Hickey and my beta and critique friends, thank you.

To my readers. Much of what you'll read has historical truth and

threads of truth woven into this story. May you find love in your

Christmas.

Chapter 1

December 1, 1955

"I hope this Christmas won't be a disaster like last Christmas was." Holly Belle Silver clasped her hands under her chin as if in prayer.

Shirley Matthews wrinkled her long nose. "What are the odds?"

"Nothing can top last year. Even if Christmas turns tragic, this holiday can't best last year's."

"Want to talk about it?"

"No. I don't want to dwell on how close to the edge of catastrophe I live. Or think about how one minute I was snug, secure, happy, and the next my world dissolved under my feet." Holly shook her head. "Or how easily calamity could happen again."

"Okay. Not a good topic for today. I'll take a rain check."

"Great." Holly glanced around the interior of *Ye Olde Queen's Inn* and smiled at her fellow waitress. "Change of subject. I love decorating for Christmas, don't you?"

Shirley shrugged. "You went ape with the decorations. They're bad news to me. More work and extra hours. It bugs me no end Charlie makes his help do all this extra work."

Holly giggled. "Charlie asked for volunteers. I'm just happy you let me come up with all the ideas while you painted your nails."

"I've got a bash after work tonight." Shirley pointed her index finger. "You fracture me, always missing out on the fun." She slapped her hands on her hips, her newly painted crimson nails flashing. "Sure you can't go with me tonight?" Her face crumpled into a wry expression. "Don't be a wet rag. Let your sitter take care of the rug rats this once."

Holly smiled and retied a red ribbon on a wreath in the window. "Rake and Randy expect me to rush home and roast marshmallows in the fireplace, make hot chocolate, and read them a Christmas story. I can't disappoint my sons."

Shirley pulled out one of the Inn's leather Captain's chairs and flopped down. "How old are they again? They're twins right?"

Holly slid into a warm leather chair across the white-clothed table from Shirley. She flipped off the old-fashioned brown pumps that accompanied her Colonial costume and wriggled her tired toes. "Yes, twins. They're eight." She propped her feet on an adjacent chair's padded seat. "Charlie hired them to act as elves during Christmas vacation." She clapped her hands. "He doesn't know what he let himself in for."

Shirley jerked off her mop cap and shook out her blonde ponytail. "Bet those two mischief makers jumped at the chance to earn a little money."

Holly inhaled the sweet, outdoorsy scent of fresh fir boughs. Much as she enjoyed the Christmas lights on the huge tree in the center of the room as well as the small trees placed around the restaurant, she frowned. "They did. But I have horrible reservations. My twins are a handful. If they break one of the hurricane lamps and set fire to this place with the candles, Charlie better have his insurance paid-up."

"What they gonna do, hand out candy canes?"

"Yes. Christmas cookies and eggnog are involved as well." Holly adjusted the red ribbon around the poinsettia centerpiece. "But both boys love the elf costumes and are raring to come work with their Mom."

"Will they dig into those Christmas stockings you hung on the fireplace mantle?"

"I'll instruct them to touch nothing except what Charlie gives them to hand to the customers."

"Think that will work?"

"Nope! They'll need straightjackets." Holly cupped a hand over her ear. "Listen, we can hear the outside music."

Muted tones of the Trapp Family Singers and *Little*

Drummer Boy floated through the windowpane. "Oh, I love Christmas and everything the giving season stands for! I love to commemorate the time when Baby Jesus was born in the stable. Such a precious—"

Shirley slapped her hands over her ears.

Holly pressed her fingers against her lips. Oops! Shirley hated her to talk about anything connected with Holly's faith.

"Time you started to look after yourself and get cooking with men again." A frown marred Shirley's pleasant face. "You still got a classy chassis and a mug to die for." She laid a warm hand over Holly's. "Don't flip your wig, but your better half's been gone two years now. Time you let go of the past and move forward." Shirley jumped to her feet and danced around the tables, her arms outstretched to embrace an imaginary partner. "Not many dreamboats steam into this restaurant, so you're gonna have to hit the road to find Mr. Dreamy."

"Shirley, I don't have time to date!" Holly sprang from her chair and joined Shirley. Felt good to let loose and dance.

When the drums to the Christmas carol faded, she padded barefoot to refold a napkin at the adjoining table, then placed the folded cloth back into the stemmed glass. "Because I love to have fun doesn't mean I'm ready to date." She placed a hand over her heart and shook her head. "I'm not."

"Okay, okay, don't get frosted. I gotta beat feet." Shirley swiped imaginary lint from the tablecloth. She gazed at Holly with a coy expression. "I could get on the horn and wrangle up some cool cats I know who'd be jazzed to date you."

"Go on to your party and have fun. Don't worry about me. When the best time rolls around, I'll meet Mr. Right." Holly smiled. "But thanks for offering."

"Hon, that kinda stuff, waiting around for a man, only happens in the flicks. Real life's no picture show." Shirley punched her shoulder. "Meanwhile back at the ranch, *we* gotta dig up that right man ourselves."

Holly skipped to the window and gazed out at the darkening street scene. Old-fashioned globe lights gleamed over happy shoppers hurrying toward home. Most of them couples. She jerked her attention back to the restaurant. "Never mind. Christmas is coming. Don't you believe in miracles?"

"Nope. We ordinary people make our own miracles. Look at me. I've been single all my life. I'm thirty years old, same as you, and no miracle has happened in this life. I attract either nerd or nowhere man. Why is that?"

"Maybe because you *don't* believe in miracles."

"Well, party pooper, let's head on upstairs and shed these threads. This costume's not the coolest duds I've ever worn."

Holly winked. "I don't know. The blue in our gowns brings out the sky-blue in your eyes." She raised her arms and swiveled her body from side to side. "And the white head-to-toe apron covers a lot of what we like to hide."

"As if you have any bad curves. But these mop caps are an absolute drag. The ugliest head coverings I've ever seen. Hides every lock of hair." Shirley smirked. "Even worse than head scarves. And my blonde halo's my best feature."

"Truer words were never spoken." Holly whipped off her mop cap, shook out her shoulder-length brown curls, and tossed her head to loosen them. She slipped the fat inch-and-a-quarter heels back onto her aching feet. "Feels good to finish for the day. I'd not noticed how my feet ache and my back hurts." She'd been too busy placing candles, wreaths, red holly berries, and lights around the restaurant, and trying not to get miffed with Shirley's lack of help. She glanced around. The Inn always looked warm and hospitable, with its wide-planked wooden floor, nicely spaced tables and chairs and floor-to-ceiling stone fireplace. But the extra Christmas candles and fir and cinnamon-scented decorations added enchantment to the scene. "It's magical, don't you think?"

"Right-o! We did a good two hours extra work. The place looks fab." Shirley undid the buttons at the nape of her white shawl, unhooked her white apron, and slid the neck-to-ankle white covering off.

Holly took one last look at her work and then clattered after Shirley up the steep flight of wooden steps to the employees' dressing area. Inside the stark room, she removed her apron and turned to let Shirley unbutton the back of her white shawl collar and her 1776 blue ankle-length gown. "I don't mind wearing this costume while I work, do you?"

"It's not so bad. Say, your family coming to spend Christmas with you?"

"Uh, no. My parents passed when I was the same age

as my twins." Holly tugged the ankle-length blue dress over her head.

"Brothers or sisters?"

"No. Just me. I have an aunt who lives in Florida." She hung the dress on a hanger and slipped it onto the clothes rack. "Someday I'd love to scrape up enough money to visit her, but I don't see that happening anytime soon. What about you? Big family?"

Shirley rolled her eyes. "And how. Four sisters and four brothers. Mom was all happy with her brood, and then I came along. The mid-life surprise. We have a blast on Christmas when we all get together. You can join us." Shirley had her dress half off but struggled to get it over her head. "I'm such a spaz. Help me, will you? I didn't unbutton this all the way."

Holly helped her untangle the dress and tug it over her head. Would she and the twins fit in at Shirley's home or would they intrude on the Holiday family gathering? "You hang eleven stockings on your fireplace mantle?" Both stood in their long Colonial petticoats.

"Yep. House gets so crammed with people and ankle biters you can't turn around without stumbling over someone."

"Sounds like fun!" No, she couldn't barge into Shirley's family over the holidays. She swallowed. Though she'd love to experience a traditional big family Christmas get-together. "Chilly up here. Sure would be nice if Charlie coaxed the owners into installing a stove."

"Won't happen. I've been working here three years, and they haven't done a thing to improve this room."

Shirley glanced around. "Not much more than an attic. Nothing here but cobwebs and clothes racks."

Holly slipped out of her long petticoat and into her own half-slip. She wiggled into her long-sleeved pink angora sweater, pulled her tweed pencil skirt over her head, tucked her sweater inside her skirt, and cinched her wide black belt around her narrow waist. She bent to slip into her black ballet slippers. "Ready?"

"Sure. Let's lay a patch." Shirley turned a waggish face to her. "We're tight, right?"

"Absolutely. You're my new best friend."

"So, like it or not, I'm hunting down that dreamboat for you and sending the two of you to the submarine races."

Holly shook her head. "Please don't. I have my hands full raising my twins. When they're grown, I *might* consider dating again. But for now, I'm too busy."

"So *you* say." Shirley winked a twinkling blue eye.

Oh brother. What did Shirley have up her sleeve? Her friend was a mover and shaker. A meddler. An enterpriser. She didn't let any grass grow under her feet when she had a scheme.

Obviously, Holly had become a project.

Holly sighed. This holiday might become a disaster after all.

Chapter 2

December 7, 1955

Holly lifted her face to the crisp late afternoon air and inhaled the scent of Christmas. How she loved this holiday.

Shirley met her at the corner and matched steps. Their ballet shoes made no noise on the cobblestones as they crossed Nicholson Street with its corner Apothecary shop and the Silversmith Shop that abutted the red brick building. Both shops were decked with bright red ribbons and green wreaths. Candles would soon light the windows.

Holly wrinkled her brow and spoke about what lodged uppermost in her mind these days. "What presents can I give the twins? Between rent, groceries, and other bills, I've got precious little money set aside."

"You'll come up with something." Shirley's concerned smile lit her plain features. "If they were girls,

I'd crochet or knit them an afghan. But your rough and tumble boys would throw one of those in the back of their closets and never think of them again...except as an embarrassment."

"Right. Rake's interested in astronomy and yearns for a telescope. Randy keeps dropping *hints* that he wants Santa to bring him a Schwinn Bike. I wish they wanted something easy like a football or baseball bat."

"Don't they have a grandmother?"

"Nope. Just my boys and me."

Shirley's grin plumped her rosy cheeks. "Meet their honorary aunt then. I'll help you buy those expensive toys. I'd hate to see those kids disappointed by Santa."

"Oh, Shirley, can you? I'll find a way to pay you b—"

"Aunties don't get paid back. I'm Aunt Shirley." She giggled. "I've been Aunty Shirley for almost as long as I can remember. Two more little nephews can't break my bank."

Holly stopped and hugged Shirley. "I knew God would find a way for my smart, mischievous twins to build great memories this Christmas."

"Sure. Every Christmas in Williamsburg is red-letter. But I doubt God is involved."

"I know He is. He's using you with your heart of gold even though you're totally unaware He is. Don't look like such a Doubting Thomas."

"Whoever that is." Shirley grinned and winked. "I've got a hunch this Christmas will be one *you'll* never forget!"

Holly mugged a face at her friend and grinned. "What else do you have up your sleeves? I don't need you to be Santa's helper on my behalf."

"Santa can't deliver all those toys to happy little boys and girls without lots of help." Shirley's blue eyes twinkled. "By the way, are those elves of yours coming to the restaurant after school today?"

"Not until next week. They're absolutely on cloud nine about spending time there with me." She poked Shirley's shoulder. "They like to be with you as well. Rake says you're a blast and a half and Randy declares you're a cool cookie."

"Yeah? Imagine that. Those two characters are boss!"

Tucking her money woes into her I'll-think-about-that-problem-later shelf in her mind, Holly's heart lightened so she almost skipped down the Duke of Gloucester Street. "Shirley, admit you love the swags and boughs of firs, magnolia leaves, and red berries draped over the doors and windowsills of all the shops. Admit you love how magical this place is at night with all the Christmas lights glowing."

"Sure. Who wouldn't love it here this time of year?" Shirley's plain face lit to almost pretty. "You've only lived in Williamsburg a few months. I love this place in all seasons. Spring brings mounds of flowers and new menus at the Inn. Tourists jam our streets in summers. Fall is glorious with gold, rust, and red colors. But this season is best, with carolers, piped-in music, and those decorations you love to use." Shirley grabbed Holly's hand and swung it between them. "Christmas is especially beautiful when we get that once-a-year snowfall."

They passed the Millner Shop. Almost passed. Holly stopped and peered in the decorated window. A scroll-filled antique sign *Just Imported From London* heralded above an array of gorgeous women's 1776 large brimmed hats decorated with masses of flowers and ribbons. A gorgeous red cloak, with luxurious white fur outlining the hood, held court at one end of the display while a collection of men's tri-cornered hats presided in the opposite corner.

Shirley tugged Holly's arm. "Come on, we'll be late."

They strode past the gunsmith, the basket maker, and the print shops without stopping to stare into the windows. The sun hung low in the west casting a golden gleam over the restored Colonial town. "I've only been here a couple months, but I love living here, working here, and raising my boys here."

Shirley nodded. "The longer you live here the more you'll love it. You were lucky to get that last apartment inside the park."

"Not luck. God's hand."

Shirley wrinkled her nose and walked faster.

Bing Crosby's *White Christmas* wafted through the streets from the town's audio system. Holly hummed along, nodding to the many visitors, hands gripping their children's on the crowded streets.

"When the fall color-show ends, guests pour in to enjoy the Christmas season. Population's building already. We're going to rake in a lot of tips tonight.

People are generous at Christmas."

Holly nodded. She would sock away any extra money until the Christmas sales began the last week of December.

The gaily painted red trolley rattled past. Smiling faces beamed from the windows. "Yesterday I noticed the Williams Market on Main Street was in full swing with a costumed group front and center singing Christmas carols. Shirley, you sing so well, you should join the carolers."

"I might someday. Now I have way too many parties to attend. Speaking of, you look like you don't have a care in the world. But I know you do."

Holly nodded. "I do. But as long as I don't think too far in the future I'm okay. Sometimes at night I can't sleep. I'm concerned I might not be able to send the boys to the College of William and Mary."

"Yeah, boys need to go to college. W & M only has about five thousand students. Between now and then, you'll get the bread. The tuition's a fraction of what other colleges cost."

"If I'm still living in Williamsburg, I'll not need to pay for a dorm room. But will the boys decide they want to major in Liberal Arts? I understand that's all the college offers." Holly sighed. "God's taken care of us since Vince died. He'll continue to care for us. He has a special heart for widows and orphans."

Shirley shot an unbelieving stare. "If thinking that makes you feel better, okay. Just don't spread that stuff around me." Then she grinned. "Besides, you don't know what fate has up his sleeve!" She smirked.

Bing finished his song and his mellow voice launched into *Silver Bells,* with Shirley's lovely soprano accompanying him.

The old-fashioned sign, *Ye Old Queen's Inn* swinging from the lamp post, welcomed them to work.

"Didn't we do a fab job with the wreaths in the windows and the fir boughs above the doorway?" Holly stood back to admire last week's work.

"Gangbusters!"

They scampered up the three steps and entered the double red doors.

"Thought you girls would be late." Charlie greeted. "Hurry on upstairs and change. I need you to punch in early tonight. We have special music and the customers are lined up inside waiting to be seated."

Holly twisted her long brown hair into a bun and thrust the tresses under her mop cap. She smoothed the apron over her bust and glanced at the patrons already seated at her station. Families. Many couples with four children. She'd wanted four, but Vince thought they could afford only two. Probably best they'd not had more, but she still yearned for a daughter. She hurried to the first table and started taking orders.

Behind her, footsteps thumping on the wooden planks announced the special musicians had arrived.

Bumping of instruments and squeaking of chairs announced they would soon play. Holly hurried from table to table. Hearing the patrons' orders over musical instruments always proved a challenge. She needed to take these orders before the group began to play.

The quartet warmed up with the usual toots and blares. But one French horn sounded louder and more insistent above the other instruments. Annoying. The flute, clarinet, and bassoon faded and then stopped playing, but the French horn kept blowing—almost like saying hello. Still annoying.

Holly turned from the family whose order she'd finished jotting on her pad and gazed at the front of the huge room. The instruments were grouped in a semicircle before the huge stone fireplace. A flute, a clarinet, a bassoon, and a French horn. The French horn blowing had become irritating. What was wrong with that musician? Why did he insist on repeating those two notes that sounded very much like hell-o? She frowned in his direction.

Then dropped the old-fashioned padded menus she held. Heavens! Could that dark-haired horn blower be Trent Conway?

The man's lank form overflowed the chair. The French horn hid the lower half of his face, but the dark-hair was different from his high school crew cut. The laughing brown eyes were unmistakable under dark brows. The straight nose she'd always admired remained newsworthy. The lean cheeks hadn't put on extra weight in the last ten years. Imagine Trent Conway here!

She waved her fingers.

He nodded and stopped playing those annoying two

notes. He flashed that smile she'd fallen in love with when she'd been too innocent to know better.

The clarinet player nodded, and the group dove into a mellow rendition of *It's Beginning To Look A Lot Like Christmas.*

Holly hurried toward the kitchen with her orders. Trent Conway! Why was he here?

Chapter 3

Holly and Shirley trudged down Duke of Gloucester Street toward the buildings where each of them rented an apartment.

"What's buzzin, cuzzin? Saw a ghost? You looked like something the cat dragged in this evening at work."

Holly nodded. She needed to talk to help clarify this new situation in her mind. "It's a long story. And not very pretty."

"Those are the best kinds. Hit me with it."

Holly drew a belly-up breath. Tonight, even the Christmas lights failed to cheer her. "You noticed the quartet that played this evening?"

"Sure. Their name's *Radioactive.* Bunch of cool-looking cats with their pegged jeans, their black-striped shirts, and their ducktails. Played good too." Shirley gave a thumbs-up, then winked. "Did you see that dreamy one who played that big brass horn? I could go for him in a big way."

"Feel free. His name's Trent Conway. We went steady during our senior year of high school."

"Cool beans!" Shirley gazed at Holly's face. "But no way I'd go out with one of your old flames." She tugged at Holly's red wool coat sleeve. "You saw a ghost from the past. I'm all ears."

Holly walked a short distance. Why not? They had time before they reached their apartments. "Okay, you asked for it." She forced a smile. "Start with two years after high school. My broken heart had almost healed when I met Vince. Haven't thought about these high school memories in years."

"That horn player broke your heart?"

"He did. I'd been expecting a proposal and a ring the summer I got a job and before Trent left our small town to attend Ohio State. He promised to write." Holly tried to sound light-hearted. "But he didn't. At all. I tried to contact him, but he'd left no address. After a year of mourning and moping, I left my job in West Liberty and found work in Columbus. I rented a room at the YWCA near Ohio State." Holly gave a rueful grin. "Since we lived in the same city now, I started each day expecting to run into or hear from Trent." She shook her head. "Neither happened. Like he'd fallen off the face of the earth."

"Why would Trent do that?" Shirley's blue eyes sparkled tears.

"I don't know." Holly smiled. "Then Vince exploded into my life like a superhero with a whirlwind romance and marriage. I almost forgot Trent."

"Way to go!"

"I thought I'd forgotten him, right? Does a girl ever forget her first love?"

"You never saw Trent again—until now?"

"Right. The last time I saw him was the day he climbed into his 1941 Ford and left for college. He kissed me and said, 'I'll always love you, Christmas Girl.'"

Shirley's blue eyes opened so wide she resembled an astonished child. "He called you that? How romantic!" She took several steps then stopped. "I wish a boy would call me something sweet."

"Trent had several nicknames for me, but that's the one he used the last time we saw each other."

"Oh, Holly, you're so lucky a boyfriend cared so much for you."

The pain certainly hadn't felt lucky. Or the years of wondering. Or the shock of running into him again with him looking even more attractive than he had in high school. "Nowheresville! I never want to see Trent again. Not now. Not ever."

"Well, you're lucky. Dream Boat Trent is *not* the one I set you up with."

"Yuck!" Holly stopped dead and grabbed Shirley's arm. "No!"

Shirley's face sported a huge grin. "Yep. Mr. Clarinet Player...and all the guys...are used to girls asking them for dates after their gigs. Groupies they call us. Anyway," Shirley's bright smile dimmed for a second, "he turned me down at first...until I pointed *you* out. Then he asked, 'When and where?'"

"You didn't, please say you didn't."

"Honey, you need to get out of that apartment and see some nightlife. Santa's bringing Mr. Clarinet Player to pick you up at seven. I'm babysitting." Shirley flashed a genuine this-will-be-so-good-for-you smile. "His name's Bob Robinson."

Chapter 4

The doorbell rang.

"Rake, will you answer that? Tell Bob I'm not quite ready. You and Randy keep him company. He's early, so he shouldn't mind." Holly slapped on some make-up foundation.

The front door opened, and a male voice rumbled. Her two sons answered in their higher-pitched voices, but she couldn't distinguish any words. She dabbed powder over her face and tugged the brush rollers from her hair, fluffed the curls out, then brushed her shoulder-length hair until her locks shone.

The conversation in the other room continued, but though she pressed her ear to the wall, she couldn't understand what was said. She hurried, but Bob had arrived thirty minutes early. She swiped on mascara, dabbed a bit of pink rouge on her pinkie and blended. Then applied *Hazel Bishop's Love That Pink* lipstick. She slipped on her nylons hooked them to her garter belt, and wriggled into her half-slip, then her ballerinas.

She slipped into the pink dress with the spaghetti straps which would take her anywhere and rushed into her small living room. "You!"

Trent rose from one wedge of her two-sectional brown couch. "Sorry, your sons just told me you're expecting a date. A guy Shirley set you up with. I'll clear out before he arrives."

Holly's hand flew to her neck. "How—?"

"I wheedled your address from Charlie. Threatened to quit *Radioactive* and split if he didn't fork it over."

"But—?"

"I know. I know. You have a million questions. By the way, you look sensational!" His chocolate eyes danced.

Trent filled her small living room with masculine aura and good will. A vase of roses set on her coffee table, tied with a Christmas ribbon and smattered with shiny green holly leaves. She managed a squeaky, "Thank you."

The boys jumped up and down, then raced from the room, their feet pounding the wooden floor of her second-story apartment.

With them gone, Trent seemed bigger than life and twice as real. All the old feelings scrambled back to strangle her.

"Those are great boys you have. Full of life. I guess the red hair comes from their dad?"

"Came," she corrected without thinking. Rioting

emotions blocked her thoughts. Her pulse sped. Her cheeks burned.

"You're divorced?" His lips, that she remembered so well, turned up at the corners like they always had. Kissable lips.

"No, Vince died two years ago. Plane crash."

His chocolate eyes lit like a kid about to taste an ice cream cone. "I'm sorry."

No, he wasn't. His face reminded her of the awed expression he'd had after their first kiss.

"Should have guessed since Bob's taking you out tonight. He's cranked. Haven't seen him so hopped up about a date in a long time."

"You knew Bob was coming?"

"Guilty. I wanted to talk with you first. Bob's got a winning way with the ladies. Wanted to warn you."

The kettle calling the pot black. "I'm capable of taking care of myself, thank you."

Trent's dancing eyes grew serious. His mouth tightened. "I also needed to figure out how to apologize. I blinked, and ten years had passed."

The doorbell rang.

She jumped.

"Must be Bob. Right on time. Usually he makes his dates wait. He's got it bad for you."

"How could he? I've never ever met Bob."

"Didn't have to. Holly, you're one in a million." Trent's wing-tips headed toward the door. He turned in her small entry to face her. "We need to talk."

The doorbell screamed again.

Holly stepped toward the door, but Trent blocked her way. "Please leave, Trent. I really have nothing to say to you. You bowed out of my life. So, please leave. Now."

The crushed expression on his face sent a knife through her heart. She shook her head. Why did he think he could step back where he left off?

The doorbell rang as if someone leaned on the bell and didn't release it.

Still, Trent didn't move.

She brushed past him and jerked open the door. A tall, handsome Swedish-type male filled her doorway.

He stepped inside, swept off his hat, and bowed. "Hello, I'm Bob." He glared at Trent as if he'd expected him to be right where he was but planned to toss him on his tail. "I take it you're leaving." Bob balled his fists. "If not, I'll give you a knuckle-sandwich."

The two tall men glared at each other.

Holly found her voice. "Heavens! Trent will you please leave, or shall I call the police?"

Trent's red face and clenched jaw and fists made her certain he counted slowly to ten. His fists uncurled. "Okay, Christmas, I'll leave." He glared at Bob. "For now."

After Trent sauntered out the door and down the hall, Bob strode inside. Holly drew in a deep breath and shut the door.

"Mom, that was boss!" Both boys yelled, totally forgetting their quiet voices.

When did they steal back into the room? She pulled in a ragged breath. "Hello, Bob. I'm Holly. I'm sorry you were part of that."

"No problem. You look fab. Ready to paint the town?"

"These are my sons, Rake and Randy." She planted an arm around each boy's shoulder. "Please shake hands and say, 'I'm glad to meet you.'"

The boys rushed Bob. Each grabbed a hand and pumped Bob's hand and arm up and down. "Glad to meet you. Glad to meet you. Glad to meet you." They screamed.

What were they doing? "Stop it boys! Behave."

A frown flashed across Bob's face. He freed his hands, straightened his tie, and rearranged his blue suit coat.

"Didn't you bring our mom a box of candy?" Rake screamed.

"All her boyfriends bring candy." Randy's voice lowered a decibel.

She frowned at them and grabbled each by a shoulder. "Boys, where are your manners?"

Bob's helpless expression almost made her laugh. Evidently, he didn't spend much time with misbehaving boys.

Randy grabbed Bob's hat and tossed the black felt to Rake.

Rake crumpled the dress hat into a ball, then dropped it at Bob's feet.

She shook each by the shoulder. "Stop acting up. At Once! Give Bob his hat."

Rake took a long time retrieving Bob's hat. He

fiddled with the tall man's shoes, then stood and handed him the hat. "Sorry."

Bob nodded, then stepped forward and fell into her arms.

She grunted with his weight, bowed under the pressure, and backstepped until she landed on the couch. Bob on top of her.

The twins laughed, patting each other on the back. One or both had tied Bob's shoelaces together.

Bob smiled, showing dimples, and buried his nose in her neck. "Mum, this is nice."

She heaved herself up but couldn't move from beneath his weight.

"This is more than I expected, but I'm game." Bob's lips moved close to hers. His breath smelled minty.

She groaned. "Please get up. You weigh a ton."

"Not quite." He pushed himself off, then held out his hand to help her up. "Thanks, boys."

She would have a major heart-to-heart with the boys when they got up tomorrow morning. They were up to something. This behavior was unacceptable.

The doorbell rang.

Holly shuddered. Not Trent again! Oh, yes. Her babysitter. She smoothed her dress, then walked as sedately as she could manage to open the door. "Come in, Shirley. You missed all the fun."

"Not *all* the fun, I hope." Bob's warm breath tickled the nape of her neck. "I'm looking forward to a lot more," he murmured.

Oh, she'd been away from the dating scene way too

long.

    She wasn't ready for this.

ANNE GREENE

Chapter 5

Holly fluffed her hair and pinned on a fascinated expression as she and Bob reigned together in the most conspicuous booth in the most expensive restaurant in Williamsburg.

She loved the surroundings with their Christmas lights and candles. She smiled and inhaled the scents of fir, vanilla, and cinnamon. A trill of pride swirled through her. Her decorations at *Ye Olde Queen's Inn* looked just as Christmassy, if not as elaborate. She would add elf dolls and angels in unexpected spots when she went to work tomorrow. Until tonight she'd not known where to best place the miniatures.

Bob proved to be an interesting and thoughtful date. He was easy to talk with. They chatted like old friends during dinner. The candles burned low as they lingered over their dessert.

Laughing together, they rushed to make the last picture show.

Inside the darkened movie theater as they watched

Rebel Without A Cause starring James Dean and Natalie Wood, Bob held her hand. Uncomfortable. Too fast for her, but he expected her to comply. So, she did. Perhaps first dates had changed in the past ten years.

Afterwards, as they strolled from the theater, a cool wind ruffled her hair. "Good flick, but I didn't fall in love with James Dean unlike half the females I hear talking at work have." Perhaps she was too old. Or too wise. Or feeling too chaotic inside dealing with a first date.

"I'll clue you in." He flashed a smile complete with deep dimples. "Natalie Wood's a show-stopper. But I had trouble watching her on the screen when I have you sitting next to me. You're incredible."

She laughed. "I understand why you have a reputation as a lady-killer." She let him take her hand as they walked toward her apartment building.

He grinned. "Where did you hear that rumor?"

"I can't reveal my sources."

"I dig you. Would his initials be TC? That bird dog wants to see me go down."

"My lips are sealed."

"Then why do *you* think I'm a lady-killer?" Bob squeezed her hand.

"You know what I like, and you treat me like a queen."

"You are a queen."

People smiled at them as they ambled hand in hand as if they were a permanent couple.

"Want a coffee or hot chocolate?"

She glanced at her watch. "No thanks, I need to get

home to the boys. They shimmy out of bed bright and early, and I promised to take them to The Craft Shop tomorrow." Holly smiled to cover her edginess. "They want to make a special Christmas present for me." Would Bob expect a good-night kiss?

He nodded. "Family first."

He hadn't said a word about how naughty her sons had behaved. "I appreciate you not mentioning how badly my sons treated you earlier this evening. I'm so sorry about how Rake and Randy acted. They're not usually so rude. Tonight was out of character for them. I've taught them better manners."

"Must be hard for them to see you interested in me. A bit of jealousy I suspect." He winked.

"You're probably right." She shrugged. Yet they hadn't misbehaved with Trent. They seemed to like him.

Maybe Bob didn't know how to interact with children. "So, you've never married?"

"Never found the right girl who could settle me down. That might have changed tonight." His smooth baritone lowered into an insinuating whisper.

Ha, what a line! "Do you enjoy your life as a musician?" Dating different women wherever his gigs landed him? Or was he ready to settle down and begin a family? She couldn't read Bob.

Which turned her thoughts to Trent. Had *he* married? She tossed her head. But she was with Bob. She must focus on him. "How long have you been a musician?"

"All my life. I play every instrument under the sun. Clarinet best. With that I lead any quartet."

"How long have you played together?"

"*Radioactive's* been together five years." He opened the door to her apartment's atrium. "Trent's new. Only been with us a month. Plays a mean French horn, but horns in on my dates too often. Pardon the pun."

"Really? Trent does that a lot?"

Bob shook his head. "Once is too much." Bob walked her upstairs to her second-floor door. He tilted her chin up and brought his lips close.

She turned her head aside. Not ready to kiss a stranger, no matter how enjoyable the date. "Um, thanks for a great time."

He kissed her cheek. "I hope this won't be the last. Our quartet plays the Inn until after Christmas. Can I see you again? Say tomorrow night?"

"I'm sorry. I don't date much. Two evenings in a row stretches my free time. My boys need me."

"I'll phone you then for next week. May I have your number?" Bob pulled his wallet from his pants pocket and unfolded a small slip of paper. He reached into his vest pocket and slipped out an expensive-looking fountain pen.

"I prefer not to give out my number." Bob was fun. He spared no expense on their date. But when she gazed into his blue eyes, Trent's chocolate brown eyes appeared in her imagination.

Bob nodded, but he flashed a frown, then concealed it with another full-court grin. "I'll meet you at work then. We play five evenings a week. Do you always work the evening shift?"

"I rotate. Three days I work early shift and three days I work evening." She didn't want him to insist on another date, so she said, "I'll see you at work."

Bob reeled her into his arms, tried for a kiss, but with her swivel, ended with a hug. "Count on it."

Trent blew a few notes into his horn. Yep, right pitch. He hunched in the folding chair Charlie provided for each of the musicians. His B flat had sounded uncertain. Not like him. He positioned the French horn across his lap and swept his gaze across the huge dining room.

No Holly yet. Maybe she wasn't working this shift tonight. He tapped his fingers over the brass valves.

Bob swaggered to his seat beside him.

Trent raised a hand in greeting.

Bob frowned and slammed down into the chair making the wood creak. "Okay, horn man, listen up!"

Horn man? Trent had expected Bob to forget the confrontation at Holly's. She had to be just another girl in a long string of girls to him.

"Get this straight! You've seen the last of Holly Silver or you're out of the quartet!" Bob loomed over him, his frown meant to intimidate.

Trent's mouth dried. He swallowed. "What?"

"Steer clear of Holly Silver. No talking. No smiling. No dates."

The hair on his neck rose. Trent pressed his rising anger down and counted to ten. Should have expected something like this from Bob. The man was a tyrant. But the clarinetist dated so many women, Trent hadn't expected any more than joking repercussions about his being in Holly's apartment last night. Bob hopped from one woman to another like a mallet over xylophone keys.

"You got my drift, Trent?"

"If I don't?" Trent tightened his fingers around the horn's bell.

"David will play your seat. Starting tonight."

Not a hard choice. He'd lost Holly once. He wouldn't lose her again. He tugged his music case over, with careful fingers removed the horn's mouthpiece and placed it into the special compartment inside the case and dug out the polish cloth. He buffed his fingerprints off the shiny brass, placed the horn inside the case, and fastened the latches. "See you around."

"Hey!"

"*You* broke our contract, Dude, not me."

"I'll sue." Red spread over Bob's face like blood pooling on a white sheet. His fists curled. "You're leaving a great gig for a girl you don't even have! Why would she choose you over me?"

"You heard him fire off that ultimatum, guys." Trent nodded to the other two players.

Both Damon and Ralph stared, open-mouthed.

Trent strode out of the restaurant into the bright Christmas lights and piped music. He could have used the extra cash, but the price tag was too high. A quick phone call from Bob and both David or Jake, though they couldn't hold a candle to his playing, would flash in to take his place, French horn in hand. *Radioactive* would start maybe fifteen minutes late. No hair off Bob's chest.

Trent sighed. He'd have to place that sign in *The Peanut Store's* window tonight.

His plan better work. He had no Plan B.

ANNE GREENE

Chapter 6

Holly matched strides with Shirley through the chilly late-night air, every jar of the sidewalk sending throbs through her ballerinas into her aching feet. She tried to concentrate on Shirley's chatter, but depression crept in.

Trent did it again. Disappeared without a word. Some other guy played French horn all evening. She'd kept expecting Trent to show, but he never did.

Spending less than a half hour in his presence had raised her hopes to heavenly expectation. Then as quickly as he'd appeared back in her life, he was gone. Again, he left no word.

She had only herself to blame for letting him rock her world. She'd promised herself never to let anyone break her heart again.

All her own fault.

Trent shattered her poor heart for a second time.

The following morning before heading to work, Holly strolled through the atrium of her apartment building. Outside the sun shone. Though the air inside smelled heavy with evergreen, and a Christmas tree in the corner blazed bright lights, her dismal heart cried.

Brakes screeched outside.

Holly sauntered to the floor-to-ceiling windows that abutted the entrance and stared outside. With another screech of brakes, a delivery truck pulled into the driveway across the street in front of Shirley's apartment. Holly rested her hands on her hips and watched through the window. Shirley ambled from her apartment to the truck while the delivery man slid the back door open. Because the truck obscured her view, Holly couldn't see Shirley, but her friend soon walked back toward her apartment, a huge grin creasing her face. She carried a red and green Christmas floral arrangement in both hands.

Fab. Did Shirley have an unknown admirer, or had she sent the flowers to herself?

Holly turned the key in her apartment mailbox, but no mail today. Not even advertisements. Her ballerinas slid over the smooth stones of the entry as she paced, waiting for the mail delivery.

A banging of the across-the-street apartment building's door distracted her. Shirley's neighbor, Paisley Robbins, minced outside and talked with the delivery driver. Holly only had a nod-and-hello acquaintance with the older lady, but she liked the woman. Paisley turned from the truck. Her neighbor carried an antique cage with some tiny birds fluttering inside.

Holly was about to journey across the street to talk with Paisley, when the delivery truck gunned out of Paisley's drive…and right into Holly's.

She sucked in a quick breath. What? She hadn't ordered anything. Maybe the truck was turning around.

But the truck pulled up, stopped, and a teenager with duck-tail styled hair jumped down.

Lucky neighbor. Someone else was getting a flower delivery. Which of her neighbors? Holly leaned against the wall to watch. She needed some joy in her life, even if the happiness came from a neighbor's enjoyment.

The delivery boy opened the door to her apartment entry. "Holly Silver?" He asked since she was alone in the entry. The boy carried a clipboard.

"Yes?"

He grinned. "Um, Miss. You got a delivery."

"Are you sure? I'm not expecting anything."

"Yep. Only problem is—um, we got a glitch in our orders. So, Gramps sent me out with these names on this clipboard, and I got packages, but I don't know which flowers go to which names."

Holly chuckled. "Got caught in the Christmas rush, did you?"

The kid nodded and backed out the door. Unlaced tennis shoes flopping on the drive, the young man hurried out to the rear of the delivery van.

Holly followed.

"Can you look at these orders and see which one yours is?" He opened the back door.

"Yes, but I can't imagine…" Holly let her words fade as the boy hauled out a huge box of chocolates in a gold package with a fancy red Christmas ribbon. The thought of a man sending candy made her heart race. The expectation such gifts brought tingled her stomach. "Is there no card?"

"No card, Miss. Do you think this candy is for you?"

She shook her head. "No. I wish it was, but I don't think so."

"These must be for you then." He pointed to an emerald vase filled with a dozen long-stemmed red roses sitting in the groove that usually held the spare tire.

She bent inside the van, stuck her nose close to a velvet bloom, and inhaled the rich rose scent. How many bouquets had she received and taken for granted? Strange, these gifts getting their cards and addresses tangled up. Was God sending a message? Was He nudging her not to turn her back on love? She'd been too afraid to risk her heart these past two years. The pain had cut so deep. But with that restraint she'd lost the joy and the excitement and the deep satisfaction of caring about someone else more than about herself and her boys. She inhaled the sweet, rose fragrance. And, the one man she wanted in her life had disappeared. Again. "No, I'm sure this one is not for me. I wonder if there is another Holly Silver in town."

"No Ma'am. We checked. And for sure, there's no other Holly Belle Silver." The teenager's voice cracked.

"I've got this one more."

Judging by his sympathetic expression, he must have seen her regret. He handed her a bouquet of bright red flowers and a vellum envelope.

Smooth and rich in her hand, the envelope's ivory paper invited her to peek inside. She glanced at the delivery boy. "This looks as if it's been opened."

"Yes, Miss. Miss Mathews and Miss Robbins opened the letter to see if it was for them. But it wasn't. I only have two more addresses. And the two other packages. Do you think this one's for you?"

She slipped the textured paper out of the envelope. Her heart fluttered. Beautiful inked calligraphy invited: *One Christmas portrait painted Sunday afternoon at Ye Olde Portrait Studio on Beacon Street.*

Tears pricked her eyelids. This couldn't be for her either. She couldn't afford to have her portrait painted. A small note at the bottom read: *Gift from a friend.* She was about to fold the note and return it to its envelope when she glimpsed a symbol in the corner—a beautiful picture of Christmas holly painted by an artistic hand.

Holly couldn't stop smiling. "Yes, thank you, this one *is* mine. This has to be my present from Shirley. She knows I have no photographs of myself, except for a few precious black and white ones from my wedding to Vince."

The kid nodded and ran his fingers though his slicked-back hair. With a hitch of his pegged jeans, a slap of tennis shoes, a door slam, and a squeal of burning rubber, the delivery truck barreled down the street.

The beautiful embossed envelope silky smooth in her fingers she decided to accept the invite. She needed her spirits lifted. Perhaps sitting for her portrait would help her forget Trent's sudden return and abrupt departure. She smiled, her feet tapped the rhythm of the lilting notes of *Winter Wonderland.*

She had to trade shifts for this Sunday afternoon, but even extra money for the sitter wouldn't keep her from accepting this surprise. Nothing would keep her from Beacon Street on Sunday. She ran upstairs to put the flowers in a vase.

She'd have her portrait painted, even if Bob Robinson had given this gift.

Even if strings were attached.

She'd face that hurdle when she encountered it.

Chapter 7

Holly turned into *The Peanut Shop* on Beacon Street. She glanced around. Why hadn't she visited here before? The place welcomed her with warm wooden floors and colorful displays. Christmas decorations overwhelmed her with red and green happiness. She sniffed the mingled scents of fir, chocolate, peanuts and sugar and spice.

Candy, sparkling every color of the rainbow, dazzled from full-length shelves lining one wall. Her mouth watered. She'd choose some for the boys. Huh, who was she kidding…and for herself? Candy always called her name. She loved any kind.

On her right, a display in tall glass jars flaunted every kind of peanut from caramel apple to chocolate covered double-dipped. She could gain weight just looking.

Fondness for this store, with every inch of the wooden walls overlaid with yummy goods to savor, could turn into addiction. She moved to a side table supporting tasting bowls filled with peanut and other exotic dips. Using pretzels as spoons, she sampled each one. Sweet, tart, and salty. She baby-stepped past baskets of other colorful goodies. If she weren't careful, she could spend her entire check here.

She inhaled a deep breath. Delightful odors teased her stomach into a rumble.

She clutched her shoulder-purse and pressed the tan leather against her body. She'd come for a different purpose. Strolling to the counter manned by a pleasant-looking white-haired lady, Holly smiled. The saleslady wore a navy colonial dress. A mop cap rode on the crown of her head, displaying her hair.

Holly made a mental note. She would try that look. Though not historically accurate, revealing hair looked far more attractive than every hair poked beneath the cap.

"What can I do for you?" The saleslady smiled, her hazel eyes crinkling her crepe skin.

"You have a sign in the window. I'm looking for the artist. Does he have a studio somewhere on the premises?"

The older lady burst into a friendly grin. "Oh yes. He's my new tenant. Just moved upstairs a few days ago." She pointed. "Head back out of the shop and enter the side door that leads to a set of stairs. His studio is upstairs." She glanced at a lollypop clock on the wall. "I'm sure he's there now. The door's not locked. Just walk on up."

Holly smiled and nodded. "Thanks. I'd like to buy a pound of this toffee peanut brittle crunch." She touched the glass above the delectable candy inside the display case. The boys would eat every smidgeon before she had a chance to taste. That worked for her figure.

As the pink-cheeked saleslady rang up her purchase, she nodded toward an intriguing display of different sized jars and bottles. "I hope you will try our variety of free samples of jams, jellies, and sauces."

"After I finish upstairs I'm returning to taste more of your wonderful products."

The lady nodded. "Do. We have such a variety of peanuts, almonds, pecans, and cashews that you'll think you'd died and gone to squirrel heaven. Our prices are extremely reasonable." The woman smiled, then turned to one of the other customers inside her crowded store.

Holly wove through the display cases and made her way to the side door. She mounted the steep incline, her insides jiggling with anticipation. Such an adventure. She'd have to puzzle-out a unique Christmas gift for Shirley.

She walked into the studio. The scent of artist oils, terpenoid, and drying canvases filled the large, sunny room. A pleasant productive-type odor. She strolled among several completed portraits, nodding and smiling, unable to resist touching one. Beautiful skin tones. Lovely poses. Shirley had chosen well. Holly clasped her hands together. This would be the highlight of her year. How could she ever repay –?

Her knees went weak. "What? You?"

The tall form unfolded from behind a large canvas. Dark hair fell over a wide forehead. Serious chocolate eyes gazed at her from under straight black brows. An artist brush, clamped between kissable lips, held a drop of crimson paint about to drip. Blue paint smudged one lean cheek. Strong fingers disengaged the brush from his mouth. His eyes warmed. Their pupils dilated making his brown eyes resemble mahogany. He laid aside the palette in his left hand and stepped forward. "Holly. I hoped you would accept my invitation and gift."

"Trent?" Her voice trembled. "You sent the invitation?"

"I thought you might remember I dabbled in art in high school."

"Oh."

"Guess you forgot." He waved a hand. "So, this is my loft. Welcome!"

"Nope. I haven't forgotten anything about you." She made a wry face. "Except your art classes. Probably because I never took any."

His brown eyes glinted. "You were too busy with your secretarial and bookkeeping studies. Did you ever use what you learned?"

Holly nodded. "I worked for several years as a legal aid in a law office but discovered I didn't enjoy being confined to a desk."

"Understood. Not my bailiwick either." Trent wiped his hands on a paint rag. "Can I get you a cup of coffee?" He turned toward an alcove where a pot of coffee perked with soothing gurgling noises.

"Yes, thank you." She needed time to let this situation sink in. Trent was an artist! This was *his* studio.

His work! "I would not have guessed our high school football star had an artistic bone in his body. That the long fingers of the star receiver could also paint beautiful likenesses of people." She gazed at his classic profile bent over the coffee machine. "Though I don't know much about art, your work looks brilliant."

His cheeks reddened. "Not brilliant." He laughed. "But pretty good for a part-time job." He handed her a white mug. "You take sugar or cream?"

"No thanks. Black."

His hand brushed hers as he passed the cup. Strong, masculine hand. Dark hair sprinkled over a wrist that extended from a faded blue shirt splashed with different types of dried oil paints, brought back memories. All exciting.

"After I finish your portrait I'd like to paint Rake and Randy. I –"

"You've changed." Her voice sounded breathless to her ears. "Not so much physically –" He looked younger than he had at her apartment or at the restaurant. So bursting with life he took her breath away. This loft was his milieu. Where he felt at home. Where he was at ease. Where he had purpose. Doing what he loved.

Her heart beat like a set of snare drums. "First the French horn and now oils." Holly's hand trembled as she brought the coffee cup to her lips and sipped. She wrinkled her nose. Trent might be a world-class horn player and artist, but he fell short on coffee making skills. She chuckled. "At least something you're not super good at."

"Yeah. Can't get the right mix of grounds. Coffee stinks." He rested both hands behind him and leaned against the coffee shelf. "I've done a lot of things I'm not super good at. But I'm a different guy now. In the past ten years I've learned not to be so arrogant and self-centered." His smile sent butterflies fluttering in her stomach. "I'm glad you came today. I owe you an apology."

"So, the portrait is an apology?" She lowered her gaze to her coffee.

"No. It's a gift. Let's call you being here a new beginning. I've gained some wisdom in the last ten years. I've learned what's important in life." He scooted closer beside her at the small counter, his hand next to hers. "These days I'm going all out for my dreams."

A sliver of fear shafted her heart. Had he changed? Was she ready for this discussion? She shook her head. Not yet. She turned her back and ambled among his paintings. "I love your work. I'm delighted to sit for you."

Waves of feelings radiated from his gorgeous body.

She moved further from his proximity. "But you must let me pay."

"A gift doesn't require payment. You accept a gift."

"I'm not sure I can accept this one. The price you charge your other clients must be high." She cleared her throat. "Perhaps I can make monthly payments."

"The price has been paid."

What did he mean? She'd paid a tremendous price in tears and regrets when he'd disappeared. But when she met Vince, she'd found happiness. What price had Trent paid? She shivered. Best let that can of worms remain closed.

"In that case, when do we start?" Had she just agreed? She really was silly. Asking for pain. And yet, before Trent disappeared she'd been a risk-taker. She'd slipped caution off like an unnecessary raincoat on a sunny day. "What is it about you that makes me want to take chances?" To throw caution to the wind. To spread her wings and fly.

"Because I believe everything is possible."

"Maybe you haven't changed as much as you think." Holly sighed. "You've always been a risk-taker."

"No. Not in some very important matters." He turned toward his painting stool. "I avoided taking one risk I always regretted. I went through a dark period after I left you. My parents convinced me not to take the biggest chance of my life." Trent situated a fresh 16 x 24 canvas on his easel. He repositioned his paint table and palette, not looking at her.

Her heart faltered, then beat double-time.

He didn't say anything. Squeezed some tubes of paint in a semi-circle around a fresh palette.

"What happened?" She bit her lip. The first time they were alone together, and she had blurted her disappointment out.

"I chose to please my parents rather than follow my heart." His brown gaze caught her and held her with a mesmerizing stare. "Mom and Dad had big dreams for me. They expected great things of their only child. A high school love didn't fit into their plans. I wouldn't admit they brow-beat me...but they did. They threatened. They bribed. They begged." He sighed. "I relented." He dipped his head and heaved another huge sigh. "I'm not proud of leaving you without a word." He crushed his empty brush on the palette. I don't deserve a second chance." His dark eyes looked as serious as death. "But will you give me one?"

Chapter 8

Holly gulped. "Are you asking me to fall in love with you again?"

"I am. I never fell out of love with you. At the end of my sophomore year when I returned home for summer vacation I planned to chuck all my parents' dreams, break their hearts, and ask you to marry me."

Holly whispered, "But you read in the newspaper that Vince and I were to be married on June 3rd."

"Exactly. I was too late." He reached out and took her hand. "If I had shown up, would you have ditched Vince and taken a second chance on me?"

Would she have? She shook her head. "No. I loved Vince. I couldn't have hurt him. I knew first hand how much a heart can be wounded. No. Not even for you."

"That's what I figured. You're brim full of loyalty. I was short on that when I left for college." He grunted. "But don't think I didn't pay a high price when I left you behind. I left my heart with you."

"I would have waited for you."

Trent nodded. "I know." He groaned. "But my parents had a college-educated girl in mind for me. You didn't fit into their plans. I'm so sorry." His cheeks flushed. "I admit I didn't have the backbone to break with them over you. I've paid that price ever since."

"Where are your parents now?"

"Still back home. Still prodding me for a grandchild. And, I think, older and wiser. They know now that what we experienced was not *puppy love*."

"Oh."

"Do you think you can give me a second chance?"

"I don't know, Trent. I have the boys now. And…and I'm not sure I trust you."

Trent groaned. "I deserve that. But I'm walking with the Lord now. He gives me the strength I lacked when I was eighteen. Though my parents never admit their mistake, they realize they were wrong to break us up. They'd be more than happy to accept you into the family. And they'd be overjoyed with Rake and Randy."

"I'm mixed up and confused, Trent. Part of my heart does flip-flops of joy. But the other part shrivels with doubt. Even looking at you and the success you've become, my mind vacillates one way and then the other. I'm a bundle of uncertainty."

"We'll take things slow. Give you time to fall in love with me again." He winked a sparkling eye. "At least I pray you will."

"That's the easy part, Trent. You're so easy to love." Holly picked at the green silk in her dress and mumbled,

"Trust is the hard part. And hurt that you never explained things to me."

Trent hung his head. "Yeah. I was a definite heel. I don't deserve your love." He raised his head and the old risk-taking, come high-water or hurricane he'd-do-what-he-needed-to-do look transformed his expression. "But miracles happen at Christmas!"

Holly nodded. "Christmas is a special time when God came down to live among us. But—"

Trent nodded. "Let's get down to business. You probably have to work today. You're wearing the perfect outfit. That green makes your eyes look like emeralds."

She glanced down at her silk dress. "This is one of my favorites."

"I need to take a couple photographs first. Then we can start." He reached for a camera on a cluttered side table.

Exactly what was she starting? A scary shiver slid down her spine.

ANNE GREENE

Chapter 9

December 15th

Holly shifted on the antique white-cushioned posing couch. Though she found holding her back straight and trying to appear relaxed fatiguing, she never tired of gazing at the artist. His mahogany eyes seemed to look right into her soul and enjoy what they found. And the way his dark hair fell over his forehead each time he bent to dip his brush into his palette made her toes tingle. She wanted to spring up and run her fingers through that well-remembered wavy hair, then smooth the unruly strands out of his eyes. The urge grew stronger each day he painted her portrait.

His gaze concentrated on the canvas. "If I remember correctly, and I'm sure I do, you were active in Christian organizations during your junior and senior years."

"Yes. And if *you* remember correctly, we met at Young Life." This was a safe subject. "I'd been a silent

Christian after I received the Lord into my life when I was a freshman. But Young Life taught me to read my Bible every day and to take all my cares to God in prayer."

"Me as well. The group was good for both of us. And?" He changed brushes and colors.

"As I learned more and more about God and the Christian life, being with other Christians grew extremely important. And talking about God came naturally."

"That's one of the many facets of your personality that attracts me. And did back then."

Holly shook her head. "No conversations about our previous attraction yet, please." Best to take this new development in her life with slow steps. Let her heart catch up with her mind. "Perhaps some other time. I'm not ready for depth yet."

His face tightened. "Okay, whatever you say."

She glanced around the studio. "You said painting's your part-time job. Is playing the horn your full-time job?"

Trent snorted. "No. Tooting's a hobby. Gets me out of the studio."

She tilted her head. "Then what's your real job?"

"I'm a detective with the Williamsburg Police Department."

She almost fell off the posing couch. "What?"

"Yep. That old risk-taking gene needed an outlet. I discovered early on after I graduated college with a business degree that I wasn't cut out for riding a desk. Or for trading stocks. Or for surgery." He held up a brush and measured something about her face. "Nope. Disappointed my folks all around."

"A detective." Holly nodded. "That sounds like you." She grinned. "I bet you're a good one."

"The best!"

"No bragging there." She smiled. "Is your job dangerous?"

"Hah. I've got stories to tell."

She nodded, tossed her head, and waved a hand. "I have the time."

"You asked for it. This is a funny one." He lifted a brush and pointed it at her. "I'll tell you about the day Santa Claus robbed a bank." Trent's brown eyes twinkled. He painted as he talked. "First case I ran that I worked undercover."

"You work undercover? In disguise?"

"Yeah. I'm on leave now. Plus vacation."

"Heavens! So much I don't know about you. You're a law enforcement officer! And a French horn player. And an artist." She frowned. "How long is your vacation?"

He squirmed and cleared his throat. "Six weeks while the department investigates me for shooting a perp. He didn't die." He grinned. "Add three more weeks for vacation." He winked, but his eyes remained serious. "Since I discovered you had moved to Williamsburg, I negotiated a vacation-with-a-purpose."

"I won't ask." Holly smoothed the concern from her face. But not from her heart. Trent had always thrived on danger. Apparently, he hadn't outgrown that quirk.

"As I was saying. My first case undercover I wore my new Resistol cowboy hat. I was assigned on a different case to this little town in Texas called Christmas. While I was there, the police discovered Helms Hillman and his four-man gang planned to rob a bank in Christmas."

"Is there really a Christmas, Texas?"

"Texas is full of cutesy town names – Surprise, Cut and Shoot, Loco, Gun Barrel City, Ding Dong, Dime Box, Jot Em Down, Turkey…"

"Okay. Sounds like fun places to visit. But how did Santa rob a bank at Christmas?"

"Our department discovered later that Helms hid behind a plastic Santa mask because his mother worked at a diner in town, and he didn't want to be recognized."

"Good reason. Not many mothers want their babies to grow up to be bank robbers."

"Or detectives. As I was saying, December twenty-third two years ago, the Hillman Gang rolled into Christmas about midday driving a stolen Buick." Trent painted furiously as he talked. "Helms hid on the floorboard until his men parked the car in the alley behind the bank. A group of kids caught sight of him and followed *Santa* into the bank as if he was the pied piper. The children kept asking for candy and presents." Trent changed brushes and squinted at his work.

"Inside the busy bank all eyes turned to Santa. The banker smiled and said, 'Hello, Santa Claus.' Then he saw the drawn guns. He froze."

"Scary."

Trent nodded, his gaze focused on his work. "One

mother, standing at a teller's window cashing a check, took one look at the guns and shoved her daughter all the way through the lobby, past the tellers, and scrammed out the back door. She grabbed her daughter by the hand, dashed to the police station, and raised the alarm."

Holly clapped her hands. "Good for her."

"Typical Texan." Trent blended two colors of paint on his palette, then dabbed his brush into the paint mixture. "Inside the bank the Hillman gang held the bankers and the customers at gunpoint. The little kids watched wide-eyed while Santa ordered the bankers and tellers to fill some potato sacks with money."

"Those poor children."

"The rest of this story could only happen in Texas." Trent lifted his brush from the canvas and flashed a grin, his mocha eyes twinkling. "As the gang headed toward the exit, Santa fired at a man peering from outside in through the front window. A hail of gunfire blasted in from the street. The Police Chief and half the town had converged on the bank. The owner of the local hardware store had emptied his shelves of guns and ammunition and passed the weapons out to the town folk. They all surrounded the bank."

"Hooray for Texas!"

"Bullets rained on the robbers like a sudden hailstorm. The four robbers herded all the customers, including the ten or so kids, to the bookkeeping room in the back, returning fire as they went. Outside, townsfolk shot hundreds of bullets through the bank's front windows. Some people staked out the back alley."

"It's a miracle none of the bank customers were hurt."

Trent nodded and waved his brush. "Santa and the robbers wrangled a hostage into the alley, and onto the Buick's back seat. Two robbers piled into the stolen car. The hostage, a young college student, slid all the way across the back seat, leaped out of the getaway car, and raced for cover."

Holly giggled. "Amazing."

"Another robber shoved two crying middle-school girls into the back seat. Running to the car, Santa shot the police chief and his deputy. A shotgun blast hit the remaining Santa's man, who collapsed into the Buick. The four robbers took off with the two girls as hostages. When they drove away, the postmaster shot out one of the rear tires. The car swerved all over the road."

"Oh. Those poor girls."

"About a minute later the car stopped in the middle of the road. Hillman discovered the gang had failed to fill the Buick with gasoline."

"You're kidding!" Holly laughed.

"There's more. Santa hopped out and waved down a passing car. The kid driving pulled his Oldsmobile over, cool as a cucumber jumped out, and sped to safety. Santa's robbers transferred all the potato sacks of money, the sobbing girls, and the bleeding robber into the stolen Oldsmobile. Once they were all finally inside, Santa discovered the fourteen-year-old driver had fled from the car carrying the keys."

Holly laughed so hard tears formed in her eyes. "A

comedy of errors. Really funny." She wiped her cheeks. "Smart kid. Dumb robbers."

"With their car stranded, Santa and the uninjured robbers ran off and hid in the brush. We arrested the bleeding bank robber lying inside the car. The girls escaped to their mamas. We fine-combed the brush and the forest but couldn't track down the gang."

"So, they got away?"

"The story's not over." Trent leaned back on the stool, his eyes laughing. "We discovered later that Santa crept back into town, stole a Ford, and slipped out of the county."

"Why is that funny?"

"Can you believe he wrecked the Ford?"

Holly shook her head. "Sounds like Santa didn't know how to drive."

"Maybe not. But wrecking the car didn't stop him. He hijacked a Dodge. The driver's father stood outside on the sidewalk feeding a parking meter and chased the fleeing car. Trying to stop Santa and get his car back, the driver's father accidentally shot his son in the arm."

"What happened to the son?"

"Santa kicked him out just before he ran the next red light."

"What did you do?"

"After that fiasco we called in the Texas Rangers. They captured the robbers at a roadblock. So, the Rangers arrested Santa on Christmas Eve."

Tears and laughter doubled Holly on the posing bench. "You're making that story up, Trent. You always could tell a tall tale."

"No. I swear. Those slapstick events happened. And the whole town did go after Santa."

"I always loved your stories. Are you sure you're not a writer in your spare time?"

"Nope. I tell stories. Love to make people laugh. But, yeah. I was in on that one. Sad to arrest Santa on Christmas Eve." Trent stuck a brush crosswise into his mouth and spoke around it. "Those kids probably never will trust Santa again."

"Oh, I have to tell the twins. They'll love this one."

"I was hoping you'd let me."

"I'm not sure I'm ready for you to see the boys again, Trent." The words popped out before she thought.

The laughter died in Trent's eyes. His shoulders drooped. He leaned forward, brush poised, but didn't touch any paint to the portrait. Then, for the next ten minutes he painted steadily without saying a word. Finally, he laid down his brushes, and picked up a slender one he hadn't used before. "I've enjoyed the last few days more than you can imagine. This is the last sitting, Holly. I hope you'll find your portrait worth waiting for." His smooth baritone sounded husky.

The deep timbre of Trent's voice sent delicious shivers to her stomach. She blinked. She hated to see Trent look so sad, but she couldn't take back her words. How could she soften the blow? "Did I mention that I have no other pictures of myself? This is truly the best present I've ever received."

He used the brush to sign his name. "No. But having

you sit for me means a lot." Trent stepped back from the easel. He straightened his shoulders and his jaw jutted. "Usually I ask clients for one sitting and then complete a portrait from photographs. But with you, I wanted to make certain I caught the real person beneath the beauty."

Heat flooded her face. "You've been sniffing terpenoid, Trent Conway. I'm not beautiful."

He propped a foot on the nearby stool, leaned an elbow on his knee, and dangled the slender brush from his fingers. "You can't see what I see. I know you. You're beautiful inside and out." The cleft in his chin stood out when he smiled.

Her face heated. "Please don't make me feel awkward with your compliments."

"No embarrassment intended. Holly, I'd like to see you more. To take you on a date."

She shook her head. "I've resisted dating for the past two years." She shrugged. But these last few weeks Shirley and the boys throw every eligible bachelor they meet at me." Holly smoothed the green silk dress where the material clung to her thighs and then flared to the floor. "Life's been crazy."

"Don't be tough on them." Twinkles again lit his eyes. "Just fit me into your schedule. By the way, I named your portrait Christmas Holly."

"Because of my dress?" Yes, she had to give him a chance or she would regret not doing so for the rest of her life. She'd learned to regret the chances she didn't take.

"Partially. But mostly because you have an inner glow that lights up my studio, reminding me of Christmas...and miracles." Trent raised an eyebrow. His lips tilted up. "You're the most beautiful woman I've ever met."

Though she'd dreamed about him for years, the timing was too soon after he popped back into her life. She stood. "I've got to go."

"Don't get upset. I'm sorry. But it's hard to keep my mouth shut. I won't say anymore."

She settled back on the couch. "I hadn't accepted any dates until I moved to Williamsburg. Instead, I dived headlong into my waitressing work, using all my energy. I love what I do."

"You dated Bob."

"I was forced into that date."

"Your friend, Shirley?"

"Right." No more dates. "When I'm ready to date again, my heart will let me know. I don't need a matchmaker. Not even a close friend like Shirley."

"But you'll miss our times together. We could begin by seeing each other as friends." Trent's voice sounded as rusty as an ancient door hinge.

"Perhaps." She wasn't ready to date the man who'd broken her heart. And from her response to his nearness, he could break her heart again. No, he could return to chasing criminals, painting portraits, and blowing his horn. Those activities should keep him out of her hair.

"I'll take that as a yes," Trent mumbled around the brush handle he'd stuck back in his mouth.

She *would* miss the engrossed expression that changed his attractive face into the artist's face. From being easy-on-the-eyes to transforming him into a man with purpose and drive and vision. She loved watching him work. Loved seeing the magic his hands created. Loved talking with him. Especially when they managed a comfortable, relaxed relationship. That's all she could handle. "Okay, friends."

The gleam returned to Trent's eyes. His shoulders straightened. "Finished. You can view the portrait now. I hope you like it."

Did he think she wouldn't? She shot up, almost afraid to look. Her stilettos tapping on the hardwood floor, she glided over to the easel.

"Well?"

She inhaled a long, deep breath. "The portrait takes my breath away. It's like looking into a mirror. I...I love the way you captured my skin tones." She touched a dry portion of the canvas. "Do I look that lovely?" Heat flooded her from her scalp to her ears. "I'm sure I'll be happy with this."

"When will you bring the boys? I'll return to full-time work in a few weeks. We need to schedule the time soon."

Trent seemed to want to connect with the boys.

She had to quit riding the fence. Did she want Trent back in her life?

Chapter 10

Holly frowned. She should be happy or at least content. But, now that the portrait hung in her rented living room above the Christmas-garland decorated mantle, she missed her mornings spent with Trent. Missed their casual conversations. Missed their spirited discussions about God and how He worked in a believer's life.

Probably missed Trent more today because a light snow had fallen on the colonial streets and Christmas lights reflected in its virginal whiteness. Because Williamsburg looked like a miracle on earth. And because Christmas was so very close. She slapped her hands on her hips. Buck up! She'd get over not seeing Trent every day.

She slipped on her coat and hurried to work.

She knocked snow off her shoes on the entryway and opened the door to *Ye Olde Queen's Inn*. The scent of pine and aroma of Christmas cooking welcomed her.

Coming to work reminded her that Trent chose to lose his place in *Radioactive* rather than stop talking with her. That had to mean something.

Shoulders back, head lifted, Holly shifted her mop cap so more curls showed and marched to her first table. Her mind still revolved with images of Trent. She dredged up a sunny smile and handed the lone occupant a menu. "How can I serve you?"

"That's a leading question coming from a beautiful girl."

The deep bass voice grabbed her attention. The man settled at her table was body-building large, handsome, and looked sure of himself. Blond crew cut, tanned skin, and bright blue eyes gazed at her with a Santa's-got-a-present-for-you expression.

A chuckle rose in her throat. "What would you like to drink? We serve our own brand of Ginger Ale. And we brew our beer using historical recipes."

"Is your coffee good?" He winked a blazing blue eye.

"Excellent."

"I'll have coffee. What do you recommend from this extensive list of colonial- era food?'

"It's all excellent. We serve traditional dishes like the Game Pye, the Hunter's Pye, and the Peanut Soup. All are tasty." She moved aside for the strolling mandolin player to linger beside the table. Rich notes of *O Little Town of Bethlehem* melted her heart. She hummed.

"Yeah, I like that carol too." The diner thrust out his

hand. "Name's John Baxter."

Holly smiled, ignored his hand, and delivered a Williamsburg curtsey. "Nice to meet you, John."

He dropped his hand and winked. "I hear you serving wenches share tidbits of colonial history with us patrons."

"We do." She tucked a finger beneath her chin and tilted her head. "I can begin with facts. Williamsburg became the capital of the Virginia Colony in 1699. Our fair village started as one of America's first planned cities suitable for becoming the capital of the largest British colony in America."

John raised a hand. "Okay. I get the history." He grinned. "And the top-notch ambiance. I dig this place being lit with candlelight rather than electricity. Décor takes me a step back in time." He fingered the pewter pepper pot and lifted the tiny spoon in the pewter salt dish. "What's this for?"

"Well, sir, salt was a major commodity in colonial days. Only the affluent could afford to buy the seasoning. So even the wealthy used salt sparingly." Holly smiled. "Thus, the tiny spoon."

John Baxter laughed longer and louder than her explanation warranted.

Uh, oh. Not just a born flirt. Another patron coming on to her. But this one looked rather interesting.

"So what entrée do you recommend?" He flashed a smile that he must know looked charming and confident.

Oh, the man was a heart-stopper. "If you have a large appetite, the Hunter Pye is enormous…jammed with venison, rabbit and duck. In his day Thomas Jefferson visited the inn. Our oyster dressing was his favorite."

"Sounds perfect. I'll take the Hunter's Pye with a side of the oyster dressing."

"I'm sure you will be pleased." Holly half-turned to leave and spoke over her shoulder. "I recommend the Applesauce Bread Pudding for dessert."

"Whatever you suggest has to be good."

She took his menu and turned toward the kitchen.

"Don't happen to know a couple boys named Rake and Randy, do you?" he bellowed.

Holly halted so fast her shoes squeaked on the wooden floor. She pivoted to face him. "You've met my sons?"

"Not only met them but teach them." He slapped a palm on the tabletop. "Those two red-haired imps ended up in my office this morning. I'm the principal of Matthew Whaley Elementary school."

"Oh, did they misbehave?" She crossed her arms. What mess had they gotten into now?

"Third time this week." His blue eyes twinkled. "So, I got suspicious. Asked them what was going on. You'll never guess."

She sighed. "With them, you're right. I never know."

"The two of them decided I would make the perfect date for your weekend."

Holly almost dropped the menu. "What?"

He hunched toward her, speaking in a low tone. "The three of us brokered a deal. They promised not to act up one more time during the rest of the school year if I ate dinner at *Ye Olde Queen's Inn* and scoped out their Mom."

"You didn't!"

"I did." John Baxter shoved his chair back and stood. "You surpassed all their superlatives." He bowed. "I am formally inviting you to take dinner with me tomorrow night, followed by an evening of ballet at *The Nutcracker*."

Holly brushed a hand across her burning cheek. "Never mind. You don't have to do that. I'll talk with the boys. They won't cause any more problems, I promise."

"A deal's a deal. You want your sons to behave the rest of the year, don't you?"

"That's blackmail."

"Come on. What's the harm? You'll enjoy dinner and love the ballet."

"Since you put my boys at risk if I don't, how can I refuse?"

"Great, I'll pick you up at 6:00."

"I live at—"

"You forget, I have all your information in my files."

Applesauce Bread Pudding

8 slices raisin bread
½ cup chunky applesauce
4 eggs
1 tablespoon sugar
1 ½ cups milk
½ teaspoon vanilla

¼ teaspoon salt
Cinnamon
Butter

Preheat oven to 350 degrees. Butter a 2-quart baking dish. Butter 2 slices of raisin bread. Cut all slices in half diagonally to make triangles and place unbuttered slices in dish. In mixing bowl beat eggs and combine remaining ingredients. Pour mixture over unbuttered bread slices in dish. Place buttered bread slices on top of mixture to decorate. Sprinkle with cinnamon. Bake covered for 30 minutes. Remove cover and bake additional 30 minutes.

Chapter 11

"Shirley, last night was wonderful." Holly stood rocking on her heels at her work station, waiting for the restaurant to open and the customers to flood in. "John's conversation at dinner was interesting and *The Nutcracker Ballet* was brilliant. I particularly enjoyed the *Waltz of the Snowflakes* and the *Pas de Deux* with the Sugar Plumb Fairy and the Prince."

Shirley's eyes were glued on the front door. "I've never seen the Nutcracker. What's it all about?"

Holly smoothed the white apron over her long dress. "The opening act takes place at a Christmas Eve party in Germany. Clara, the little daughter, receives a special gift. A nutcracker. Clara loves the nutcracker, but her brother Fritz breaks the toy."

"Just like a boy."

Holly nodded. "Clara lays the nutcracker in her doll bed so it will get well." Holly's memory came alive as she talked. "The party ends. Clara and her family go to bed. Clara sleeps, then gets up to make certain her nutcracker is resting." Holly can't resist pirouetting around the dining room. "The dolls and toys all wake to life. Mice run around the nursery. The nutcracker fights the mouse king and loses. Clara throws her slipper at the mouse king and saves the nutcracker's life." Holly performed a Plié. "The nutcracker transforms into a human prince." Holly mimicked an Arabesque as well as she could in her long gown.

Shirley stared wide-eyed. "Now you're cooking!" She clasped Holly around her waist and twirled with her. "I could fall in love with a nutcracker prince."

"Everyone does. So, then the prince and Clara set off through the snowy woods for the Land of Sweets where the beautiful Sugar Plum Fairy rules. The fairy orders coffee, tea, chocolate and the Russians to dance. The flowers and the Sugar Plum Fairy dance. The ballet ends with everyone dancing." Holly was breathless from her moves.

Shirley scooted off to wait her first table. Order taken she hustled back, her eyes bright. "That plot doesn't make sense."

"You're right. Not much plot. The ballet's about beautiful dancing and out-of-this-world music. These days no one cares that the plot is weak. The Nutcracker's a Christmas tradition." Holly rushed off to serve her first table.

The family ordered the special molasses cookies and hot cider. After she delivered the sweets and drinks, Holly scurried to Shirley's side. "John Baxter said that when the ballet was written critics chastised Tchaikovsky for writing music to accompany such a flimsy plot. The composer had already received acclaim for his music for the *Sleeping Beauty* and *Swan Lake* ballets."

"Your John Baxter turned out to be an egghead, eh?"

"Why not? He *is* Rake and Randy's school principal."

"You liked John?"

"Well, yes. But I felt strained while I was with him because John only sees the boys when they misbehave." Holly shook her head so her brown curls bounced under the mop cap. "Which they haven't done until the last few weeks after they cooked up the scheme to fix John up on a blind date with me."

"From what I saw of the guy at your table a couple nights ago, those rug rats of yours spotted a winner. He's cowabunga! How does he compare to Bob Robinson?"

Holly glanced at the few customers arriving. Except for the family enjoying the cookies, her tables were still empty. Wouldn't hurt to take the work time to answer Shirley, since her friend had set up her date with Bob. She took Shirley's hand. "I'm sorry. I didn't like Bob's aggressive attitude. I really didn't like that he gave Trent Conway an ultimatum."

"Yeah, Bob did seem overbearing. I'm all ears. What ultimatum?"

"Bob told Trent never to speak to me or see me again. If Trent did, Bob would fire him from *Radioactive*."

"Wow. That's heavy. I noticed Trent doesn't play with the band anymore. So, I'm guessing there won't be any more dates with Bob."

"Correct."

Her other tables remained empty. Shirley had serviced her table. Holly had time for more girl talk. "I told you about the portrait Trent painted."

Shirley nodded. "So, to rephrase. How does John Baxter stack up next to Trent Conway?"

"I honestly don't know." Holly rubbed the back of her neck. "Last night, when the Prince entered the stage to dance with the Sugar Plum Fairy, my thoughts jumped to Trent…even though John sat beside me holding my hand."

"Wow! Sinister. Are you going to see John again?"

"I don't know. I'd hate to get involved with him and then sometime in the future break-up. I don't want to hurt him. And John might take his injured feelings out on the boys."

"You're kidding, right?"

Holly frowned. "Partly. But I don't want to chance that happening."

"What about Mr. Artist? Will you see him again?"

"I don't know. He totes a lot of baggage and memories with him. I'm not sure I can handle letting him carry all that back into my life."

"Why don't you admit it, Holly? You're stuck on Trent again. He's your Mr. Dreamy."

"How can I? I'm afraid I'll get hurt again."

"One way to find out. Take a chance! With that dreamboat, I would."

Holly walked to her empty table and whisked a damp cloth across the top, gathering crumbs from the molasses cookies. Did she have the nerve?

Colonial Molasses Cookies

Heat oven to 360 degrees
4 ½ cups all purpose flour
4 teaspoons ground ginger
2 teaspoons baking soda
1 ½ teaspoons ground cinnamon
1 teaspoon ground cloves
¼ teaspoon salt
1 ½ cups shortening
2 cups sugar
2 eggs
½ cup molasses
¾ cup coarse sugar

Mix together flour, ginger, soda, cinnamon, cloves, and salt. Set aside.

In a large mixing bowl beat shortening until softened. Gradually add the 2 cups sugar, beat until fluffy. Add eggs and molasses, beat well. Add half the flour mixture, beat until, combined. Stir in remaining flour with a wooden spoon. Shape dough into 1-inch balls. Roll in coarse sugar. Place on ungreased cookie sheet 2 inches apart. Bake in a 350-degree oven 12 to 14 minutes until light brown and puffed. Let stand 2 minutes and transfer to a plate.

A half hour later Holly grinned and stood shoulders

back, head held high. These were her pride and joy.

"Hi, Mom." Rake shouted from across the room as he pranced toward her, his elf shoes slapping the floor.

"Ready for work, Mom!" Randy pushed against Rake in his attempt to reach her first. Rake sprawled, almost hit the floor but regained his balance, and shoved Randy, managing to grab her around the waist seconds before Randy.

"No roughhousing boys." Holly touched her finger to her lips. "Shush. In here we use our quiet voices."

"Look what Mr. Charlie gave us to hand out." Rake opened the decorated Christmas bag he held and showed her the treasure inside. "Candy canes!"

"Wonderful." She selected one and tucked the cellophane-wrapped red and white striped cane onto her apron bib.

"And look, Mom!" Randy displayed a large platter of red and green iced sugar cookies baked in the shape of angels.

"Brother, that was some miracle. Those cookies almost landed on the floor!" Shirley whistled.

"Okay boys. Elves are quiet and soft-footed. They pop up at your side when people aren't looking and surprise them. They do not make loud noises and shove one another." Holly smiled at the identical red-heads with their sprinkles of freckles over pert noses."

Two pairs of hazel eyes gazed at her with naked love. Both heads bobbed *yes* making the green caps with their funnel tops shake and the bell atop jingle. Green felt elf shoes with curled up tips shuffled on the wooden floor.

"Hey guys, those red-striped tights look groovy. I could tell you were elves in the dark." Shirley patted Randy on the back. "You two glow like neon lights."

Charlie walked into the dining room. "Okay boys. No shenanigans or your first day will be your last. Circulate around the room and hand out the treats to people seated at the tables as well as those waiting in the anti-room to be seated." He grinned at Holly. "And if I find sticky fingers, you won't be able to carry any left-overs home tonight."

The boys straightened and put on their obedient faces. "Yes Mr. Charlie. We are elves, not boys. And no sticky fingers. You can count on us."

Holly trembled. This had seemed like a good idea when Charlie approached her. She'd have to keep a strict eye on the boys. In their eagerness, they could burn down the restaurant.

She sighed. But they did look cute. And she loved having them near. She watched her delightful little elves weave between the tables gaining laughs and small talk from the patrons. They were adorable. How long would that behavior last?

ANNE GREENE

Chapter 12

Trent cleaned his brushes. Soothing. Relaxing. Freed his mind to think about important things. After Christmas, his full-time job waited for him. He swirled a brush in terpenoid and watched the red paint whirl in circles until it disappeared. He laid the brush aside.

He had to step up his campaign.

At some point he'd have to confess to Holly. Suck in the embarrassment. Take his bitter medicine. Force out words that had been stuck in his throat. How time flew. He blinked his eyes, and ten years had disappeared.

He cleaned another brush. Sure, by some standards he'd been successful. He'd joined the Williamsburg Police Force and worked his way up to detective. Not much crime, and with time on his hands, he'd created Trent Conway's Portraits. He'd fallen into the brass-playing gigs by accident.

Life was good. He had friends. Enjoyed his work.

Hadn't realized how huge a gash his divorce had torn in his life. He pulled the brush from the terpenoid and worked the paint-clogged threads through the artist's soap.

When Holly moved into her apartment in Colonial Williamsburg his good life ground to dust. Became colorless and dead without the woman he'd fallen in love with in high school.

He rinsed the brush in warm water, squeezing the sable strands between his fingers. How had he fallen into such a trap? Older and wiser now and after the fact. Hindsight. He should have never let her go. He set the brush bristles up in the drying rack.

Even after he confessed, would she take him back? Did she still have feelings for him? If possible, Holly was more beautiful today than she had been those quickly-evaporated years ago. And love for her boys had strengthened her. She had grown into a nurturing woman.

What now? The Holly he'd known would never be interested in a player like Bob Robinson. And she didn't seem to have changed. Bob would be no problem.

But that school principal Rake and Randy set her up with looked like serious competition.

He smacked a fist into the palm of his other hand. "I've got to make my move!"

He stored his brushes and paints, pulled on his leather jacket and clambered down the stairs.

Ye Olde Queen's Inn hummed with couples and families. He stood in the receiving area waiting for a seat. *Radioactive* played in front of the stone fireplace. Trent's fingers moved over invisible brass keys along with the notes the quartet played. He hummed *I'll be Home for Christmas.*

He grinned. If he'd ever imagined elves, Rake and Randy personified the mischievous wee folk. The two darted, slithered, and pranced in and out between the tables. Good touch, Charlie. Who could resist returning to the restaurant to watch the elves as much as to enjoy the food?

Randy rushed over. "Have a cookie, Mr. Trent. They're real good."

Trent selected a red-iced angel and touched a thumb to the corner of Randy's mouth to swipe off a few red and green crumbs. "Thanks, Randy."

"Mr. Trent, you and Mom are the only two grown-ups who can tell me from Rake. How do you do it?" Wide hazel eyes above rosy cheeks questioned him as if the safety of the world depended on his answer.

"Easy, Randy. You're a shade heavier than Rake. And your mouth is shaped differently. More like your mom's." Trent ruffled Randy's hair. "Your hair isn't quite as red as Rake's. You look alike, but you're different. Unique. You're your own man."

Randy's chest puffed out, and he stiffened his back. "Mom says we both look like Dad."

"I never met your dad. But you and Rake have different expressions from one another. You look at life in unique ways. You're the impetuous one and Rake's the quieter one." He tilted Randy's chin up. "It's easy to tell you from your brother."

"Thanks, Mr. Trent. You're the greatest!"

"You better get circulating or Charlie will give you the evil eye."

"Right!" Randy saluted, making his elf's hat tilt and turned back to dance among the tables and offer his cookies. His bell jingled with every step.

Across the room, Rake waved some candy canes and frolicked over. "Here's one for you, Mr. Trent."

He knew Holly hadn't missed the boys' greeting him. She carried a load of empty dishes from a vacated table and glided in his direction.

Now or never. Trent gulped.

Holly approached, looking sweet and more delectable than any food the restaurant served. She smiled. "Hi."

"Great boys you have there! Can I take you to the Christmas Tree Lighting tomorrow night?"

She blinked her big emerald eyes, hesitated, then said, "Okay. I'm off work. What time?"

"I'm not sure when the festivities start. Early I think. I'll pick you up at four."

"Perfect. I'll see you then." She hustled toward the kitchen.

Wow. Ten years erased in a few seconds. She'd said *yes* and looked elated. The tension binding his chest disappeared.

A shoulder bumped his and almost knocked him against an older lady standing next to him.

"Look where you're going!" Trent glimpsed John Baxter moving through the crowded entry toward a table on Holly's side.

Trent grinned. Appeared he'd arrived just in time. Seemed Baxter was after the woman he loved.

Chapter 13

"Remember the time after junior prom that you and I drove to the lake?" Trent squeezed Holly's hand and led her toward the huge Christmas tree in the center of Market Square.

"That was fun. A night to remember." Holly snugged her red coat under her chin and shivered.

"But you were chicken."

"Yeah. But you egged on Ginger and Dick. You talked them into swimming in that dark water. You wanted me to jump in too."

"I was wild and crazy in those days."

"You were. I wasn't about to skinny dip in Rogers Lake with the car headlights spotlighting me." Holly laughed. "Although I did want to see what you looked like under that white tux jacket."

"If the headlights hadn't been shining on the lake, would you have gone in?" Best not to mention how much he'd wanted her to jump in. But he needed to keep her talking about the happy times they'd shared. Remind her how much they'd cared about one another.

"No. I wasn't about to dive into that dark water. Or get my formal messed."

"Remember –."

The piping of fifes and the snare of drums interrupted, drowning his words. Marchers approached, dressed in colonial garb, and high-stepped down the cobblestone street.

Crowds on both sides of the street clapped and cheered, then fell in behind the loud band as they led the way to the giant Christmas tree in the center of the square.

Holly's hand nestled warm in his as they joined the hundreds of people, boots and shoes clattering over the cobblestones, headed toward Market Square. For the first time in ten years his world tilted to its right spot. He whispered, "You're the only woman in the universe for me." Apparently, she couldn't hear over the band piping and the drums drumming. "You fill the empty vacuum inside my heart."

For good or ill, he didn't know which, the band and crowd noise overwhelmed his words. Her eager expression didn't change. With her nose and cheeks tipped red from the cold she gazed at the festive scene, her head tilted back, a happy smile on her lips.

They arrived in time to see the dark, giant spruce spring to life with lights. The tree illuminated joy on the faces of the surrounding people, especially the children.

The drums faded, and the fifes burst into *O Come All*

Ye Faithful.

As if led by a choir director, the bystanders merged their voices in singing the beautiful carol. Afterward the fifes played, and they all sang some of the other loved Christmas carols.

With the ringing of sleigh bells, Santa and Mrs. Claus arrived on a horse-drawn carriage. With screams of delight, the noisy, jumping children surrounded the horses, the carriage, and the red-suited couple. He'd invited Rake and Randy, but the twins were attending a birthday party for one of their school friends.

Holly's hand chilled inside his. "Let's go to Rudy's for a wassail or a hot chocolate. It's getting colder."

"Hot chocolate for me." She grinned, her cheeks rosy, and her emerald eyes ablaze.

He steered her down a cobblestone lane. Lampposts strung around with fresh pine branches lit their way until they arrived at the small bakery. "We can watch the fireworks above the Governor's Palace from here." He pulled out a chair at one of the two sidewalk tables for her. "Knowing about this place is one of the benefits of living here."

She smiled. "One of the many. I can't believe I'm spending Christmas in Williamsburg. This place is so romantic."

He counted on the romantic ambiance. They settled at a sidewalk table cupping the warm drinks in their cold hands.

Soon cascades of fireworks exploded in the sky outlining the mansion, the trees and the gardens.

They oohed and awed together.

As red and green tints from the explosions lit her profile, he yearned to reach across the table and touch her soft cheek. Over the years, he'd missed her more than the ache in his heart laid bare.

She gazed at the sky, unaware of his pain, her expression as joyful as a child's.

He reached across and cradled her hand inside his.

After the fireworks climaxed into a giant crescendo, they stood and strolled past a turned-up keg of roasted chestnuts. He stopped and bought a bag from the vendor. They shared the warm nuts as they strolled the festive square.

"Are you cold?"

She nodded.

"Ready to go home?"

She shook her head.

"Let's stop here for another drink."

"Sounds like fun."

He slipped a five into the waiter's hand. The man led the way inside to a table for two beside the roaring fire.

"I love this coffeehouse."

"Yeah, Carlton's is the best." He seated her and ordered two hot scones with butter and two more cups of hot chocolate with chocolate stirrers.

"This has been an unforgettable evening."

Her smile sent ripples through his stomach. "Want to take in the Christmas Homes Tour with me? The ramble takes place all next week. When do you have a day off?"

"I do have Wednesday off work." She played with

the top button on her wool coat. "What happens on the tour?"

"The garden club sponsors the event. Home owners in the historic district open the doors to their private residences, and the public pays to stroll through their homes. The décor is Colonial. The decorations Christmas. The gardens behind each home are opened. As well as the sheep, hogs, and goat pens." Trent fiddled with his hot chocolate spoon. He swallowed. Would she want to see him again?

"Sounds delightful."

He breathed again. "Okay, Wednesday at two. We could take in a movie after."

"Hmm, Trent. Are you trying to monopolize my time?" She raised the cup to her lips.

"You guessed it. You still know the way I operate. How about the tour?"

"Sounds too lovely to miss."

"Great, two o'clock." He sipped his hot chocolate. Then said, "Hey, do you remember the time I took you rowing on Lake Rogers? You splashed me and soaked my jeans and shirt from head to foot."

"I did." She smiled.

"And I developed blisters on top of blisters on both palms from all that rowing. Couldn't afford to rent a power boat."

They laughed.

"Remember how exotic the gym looked when we had the Cinderella prom theme with the stars and the Disney carriage? Junior year wasn't it?"

"How could I forget? You looked so handsome in your white tux jacket and I wore my red strapless ballerina dress."

"Did I?"

"You were always handsome. Still are."

"You're even more beautiful than you were then. We have closets filled with great memories. Two years of knowing one another."

"Yes, I never looked at another guy."

He took her hand in both of his. "I loved you then and I love you now."

She squirmed and gazed at the door. "We have to leave. The boys will be home from the party soon." She rose and gathered her shoulder bag, a frown marring her smooth forehead. "I trusted you then. Now I don't."

Trent groaned. "What can I do to regain your trust?"

"I'm not sure you can."

Chapter 14

December 20, 1955

"Oh, Trent, thank you. I've always wanted to take this carriage ride around Williamsburg." Holly grasped the hand Trent held out and ascended the three steps into the bouncy carriage and settled on the padded seat.

Trent mounted behind her and perched beside her, his thigh touching hers. He casually laid his arm across the seat behind her.

Joy tripped through her heart. She tugged her red knit cap down around her ears to shut out the cool breeze.

"Giddup." The driver urged his horses.

The carriage lurched forward with Trent's hand grasping her shoulder, holding her steady, until the ride smoothed into a slightly rocking motion as the coach jounced over the cobblestone street.

"I enjoyed our tour of Christmas homes. It was fascinating. So many of the owners shared the history of their homes. I loved strolling through the back-yard gardens, even though most of the vegetation was dormant." Holly gazed at the colonial shops the horses clopped past. "To say I'm impressed with how self-sufficient the people in colonial America were is putting it mildly." Holly bounced on the seat. "Everything any resident needed he grew in his own backyard or the item was manufactured somewhere inside the village. No imports."

They rolled past the cabinetmaker and the cooper. "Like at those shops." She pointed.

"Not many imports anyway." Trent cleared his throat. "Not much money in those days. People bartered for goods they didn't make or grow themselves."

The colonial houses slowly slid by. Almost, she could believe she lived in those by-gone days. They passed the working black-smith shop, with its roaring fire, and the muscular blacksmith in his big leather apron hefting his hammer up and down to clang on the anvil. The blacksmith pounded on something glowing red hot atop the anvil. Holly removed her fingers from her ears once they'd glided by the gunsmith and the silversmith shops.

The carriage turned onto a one-lane dirt road and drove past double-story white-frame houses surrounded with picket fences. They breezed past the book bindery.

"Only the rich could afford books." Trent nodded toward the bindery window.

"That's sad. I love to read. Do you still read much?"

"Mostly historical books and books about politics." Trent shook his head, his dark hair unruly in the breeze. "If Americans don't study our history, we're doomed to repeat the worst part. Knowledge is power." He ran his free hand through his hair. "Don't get me started. I get pretty loud in my opinions."

"I couldn't agree more about knowing history. This is the right place to visit." She gazed into Trent's serious brown eyes. Why was he so intense today? He'd seen these places countless times. What was bugging him? The further they rode, the more edgy he appeared.

As they rolled past, Trent pointed to the brick yard. "Even today this establishment produces bricks for some of the homes."

"Amazing."

He was silent as they drove down another dirt road. The muscles in his arm lying across her shoulders tightened. Something bothered him. Something he'd been thinking about since they settled inside the carriage. "Is anything wrong?"

"Holly, I have something I've been wanting to confess. It's been eating me."

"Oh?" Darn. She didn't want any deep discussions. Wanted to enjoy this ride and not think. Just snug here, warm and comfy, and enjoy the sights and feel the chill wind on her cheeks.

"I was married."

Her heart jolted. She shouldn't be surprised. Trent was handsome, personable, and as far as she could tell, made a reasonable living with his two jobs. She threw back her head and inhaled the crisp morning air. Sunshine warmed her back while the cool breeze chilled her cheeks. She stiffened her courage. She could handle this. "Okay."

"My senior year at college I married the girl Mom and Dad all but shoved in my face. Julie was pretty, intelligent, and already a rising star in the political world, thanks to her Senator father."

"So, you made your parents happy." She forced life into her flat voice.

"I was wrong to marry Julie. I loved you."

"What happened?" Was Trent over his marriage with Julie or did he still hold feelings for her?

"Our marriage lasted less than six months. Turned out I wasn't what Julie wanted in a husband." Trent shook his head. "I had no interest in relocating to D.C. Nor was I eager to support Julie in her political career with all the parties, meetings, and back-biting." His hand slipped down further and clasped her shoulders. "We have differing political views as well."

"No. You wouldn't thrive living that sort of life. You've never had an easy time keeping your mouth shut when you disagreed with someone's opinion." Holly gazed into the street. At least the old Trent would have hated the political life.

"The straw that broke our marriage happened one night when I asked her if she planned to have children." His smooth voice sounded strained as if he spoke through a tight throat. "We should have ironed that out before we rushed into marriage."

"Oh?"

"Children weren't included in her life plan. I discovered Julie had a high-walled, unbendable life plan. The husband she had in mind was wall-paper. Decoration."

"I'm so sorry."

"Then somehow she discovered I was still in love with you. I don't think that made a lot of difference to her." Trent's voice turned hard. "Julie didn't care who I loved. For her political alliances she entertained quite a number of men. Flirted with them all. Part of her job description Julie explained."

"I made excuses for her, not wanting to accept her behavior." Trent's warm hand squeezed her shoulder. "But, when I joined the police department, she divorced me." He gazed straight ahead. "Police work didn't meet her social standards."

Holly laid a hand on his. The one clasping her shoulder. "So, after your divorce, you remained single all these years?"

He nodded. "Filled my life with my careers and serving the Lord when I could." He tightened his grasp around her shoulders until he hugged her to his side.

She didn't resist or take her hand off his. They rode in silence, his words revolving inside her mind. "Danger and excitement belong in your life. I can't see you happy without them."

"And children. I want a pack of kids. A whole house full." He grinned. "I wouldn't wish being an only child on anyone." He grinned as if he'd unburdened his thoughts and could relax. "Your two make a nice beginning."

She pulled away to stare at him full in the face. "But you chose the life your parents planned for you."

"Yes. I'm older and wiser now." He put his arm around her again. "And so are Mom and Dad."

She snuggled into his side. "Aren't we all." He'd obviously found telling her to be difficult. Listening had been hard as well. Raised more questions. "Your Mom and Dad won't interfere with your life again?"

His voice smoothed into its usual baritone richness. "I can't promise that. When I take you to meet them, and you know I must, they'll fall in love with Rake and Randy and pressure me to marry you."

"Doesn't sound like they are older and wiser."

His deep laugh rang out. "Their pressure will be more subtle. They remind me constantly that they aren't getting any younger."

The carriage jolted to a halt, back at the sidewalk stop where they had started. "Okay, folks. Hope you enjoyed the ride." The driver tipped his top hat.

"We did." Trent hopped out and helped her down. He caught her hand and they strolled down Duke of Gloucester Street.

Holly's heart still beat double-time. Trent had spilled his heart. What should she do?

Chapter 15

Holly gazed out her apartment window at the dusting of snow sparkling in the early morning dawn on the cobblestone street below. She sipped the hot cider in her cup and tried to still her wild thinking.

Trent stirred her emotions like no other man ever had. Not even Vince. She'd loved Vince with all her heart and they had rejoiced together when their babies were born. Though they'd only had a few years with one another, they'd loved well…until the day the bottom dropped out of her world when the plane crashed. She'd spent two years grieving Vince's death.

Time to close that chapter of her life and flip open a new one. Judging from her sons' actions, they hankered for a complete family again. They yearned for a father.

She paced the small living room, circling the perimeter over and over.

Would Rake and Randy be hurt if she stopped any romance from developing between her and their principal? John was a fine man. If Trent hadn't entered her life again, she would be tempted to further her relationship with John. But her heart already seemed to be taken. Had she ever stopped loving Trent?

She paced, stopping now and again to sip the cider.

She'd already refused one date with John. She'd be up front with him. The sooner the better. The handsome, personable man would have no trouble finding a woman whose heart was not already taken.

Trent had spent eight of the last ten years of his life alone because he loved her, and he'd not made contact because she was married. Then he'd given her time to grieve before introducing himself with that French horn. Leave it to Trent to be creative.

When she spent time with him all the old feelings flooded her with new strength. Now she hated to be away from him.

Trent was older and wiser to the point that he knew how his parents would react if she agreed to meet with them again. How could she not trust him considering his actions during the past years?

Her old love made her heart sing again. Caused joy to pulse through her veins. She adored watching him interact with the boys. Trent seemed smitten with the twins. The boys jabbered less and less about John and more and more about Trent. That meant something.

"The signs of love are all in place. Thank You, Lord. I hear what You're saying. Shirley and my sons are misguided matchmakers. You brought Trent and me together in high school and again in this beautiful city

I've grown to love. I'll trust You and will no longer turn my back on the promise of love."

Her telephone rang.

"Oh, hello Trent." Butterflies flitted inside her stomach.

"How about you go to church with me tonight? I guarantee Rake and Randy will love it. The children are performing a pageant."

"Three days before Christmas?"

"A time to be together with loved ones."

Could she get the time off from work? "I don't know."

"The boys will love it."

Trent picked her up at her apartment. The boys were angels, each hanging onto one of Trent's hands, laughing and joking with him. No bad behavior.

She rushed into the bathroom to touch-up her lipstick.

Randy tip-toed in. "Mom."

"What dear?"

He inched over and fingered her powder and the nail polish cluttering the sink's ledge. "Rake and I don't care if you choose Mr. Trent over Mr. John. We like Mr. Trent a lot and really, really want to have a new father." He thrust a small arm around her neck. "We miss Dad." He kissed her on the cheek leaving a tiny wet spot. "But Dad's in heaven and having a good time taking care of kids up there. We need a Dad, so we can have a good time down here."

Holly nodded, crooked his small body in her arms, and kissed his cheek. "Thank you, sweetie!"

"Besides, it's too hard not to get into trouble at school." Randy broke from her arms and whirled in a circle. "And we don't want the principal telling us we're bad at school *and* at home." He giggled and darted from the room.

Holly smiled, gathered her purse and coat, and the four of them left her apartment.

They sat together in church. She and Trent sandwiched the boys between them. Shirley slipped in and established herself in the vacant seat Holly saved beside her.

Contentment stretched over her as strong and sweet as the taffy pulled in the Williamsburg Candy Shop.

As the pageant progressed, all three of the males in her life wore an engrossed expression. Rake nestled close to Trent and Trent had his arm around her son's shoulder.

"Look at that yummy narrator." Shirley whispered loud enough the narrator's cheeks reddened. "He's just the type of hunky male I could go for."

The children filing in and taking their places on the church's small stage quieted Shirley.

The tall narrator straightened his blue robe, cleared his throat, and began speaking. "And Joseph also went up from Galilee, out of the city of Nazareth, into Judea, unto the city of David, which is called Bethlehem; because he was of the house and lineage of David to be taxed with Mary his espoused wife, being great with child. And so it was, that, while they were there, the days were accomplished that she should be delivered. And she brought forth her firstborn son, and wrapped him in swaddling clothes, and laid him in a manager, because there was no room for them in the inn."

The small girl playing Mary cradled the doll in her arms and sweetly hummed.

"And there were in the same country shepherds abiding in the field, keeping watch over their flocks by night."

Three small shepherds filed in, holding staffs, and checking the audience for their parents.

"And lo, the angel of the Lord came upon them, and the glory of the Lord shone round about them; and they were sore afraid."

A small angel with a tilted gold halo hurried down the aisle and joined the shepherds on stage.

"And the angel said unto them, Fear not: for behold, I bring you good tidings of great joy, which shall be to all people. For unto you is born this day in the city of David a Savior, which is Christ the Lord. And this shall be a sign unto you; Ye shall find the babe wrapped in swaddling clothes, lying in a manger."

Other small angels filed up onto the stage, sometimes brushing their wings against one another by mistake. Small giggles mingled with the narrator's words.

"And suddenly there was with the angel a multitude of the heavenly host praising God, and saying, Glory to God in the highest, and on earth peace, good will toward men."

The crowded stage overflowed with shining small

faces grinning into the audience and searching for parents.

"And it came to pass, as the angels were gone away from them into heaven, the shepherds said one to another, let us now go even unto Bethlehem, and see this thing which is come to pass, which the Lord hath made known unto us."

Small hands waved from the stage. Small angels and shepherds jostled one another as they crossed the stage to stand in front of the living manger scene.

"And they came with haste, and found Mary, and Joseph, and the babe lying in a manger. And when they had seen it, they made known abroad the saying which was told them concerning this child. And all they that heard it wondered at those things which were told them by the shepherds."

Caught up in the story, the children quieted and some of the shepherds knelt before the mother and baby.

"But Mary kept all these things and pondered them in her heart. And the shepherds returned, glorifying and praising God for all the things that they had heard and seen, as it was told unto them. Luke 2:4-20"

The audience stood to their feet and clapped long and loud for their children. The narrator bowed. The organ played, and all the parents surged to the front of the church to grasp the hand of a small angel, shepherd, or Mary or Joseph.

Laughter and voices mingled.

The tall narrator, his blue robes flowing behind him, pushed through the crowd and strolled over to Shirley.

He offered his hand and smiled. "Hello, I'm Seth Johnson. I couldn't help noticing your face in the crowd. I've seen you working at *Ye Olde Queen's Inn* and have been wanting to meet you. That last shaft of sunlight beamed on your golden hair, and I took that for a sign that you might agree to join me for a cup of hot chocolate." He glanced at Holly. "That is, if your friends don't mind."

Shirley beamed, shook Seth's outstretched hand, and nodded. Her voice sounded breathless. "Yes, I'd love to share a hot chocolate with you." She gazed down at her shoes. "I've noticed you eating at one of my tables now and again."

She glanced at Holly, her plain face lit from within giving luminous sweetness to her features. "Do you mind?"

"Of course not. The Village Café is open until all hours. Go. Enjoy." Holly smiled at the tall, rugged-looking narrator. "I know you'll take good care of my friend." She glanced at the manger scene where Mary still held the baby in her arms. "I've discovered miracles still do happen at Christmas."

Seth's deep laugh rang out, "Yep. They do that." He put a hand on Shirley's back and guided her through the crowd. "Did you receive the Christmas flowers I sent you?"

"Yes. But I didn't know you sent them. The flower shop had a mishap with whose flowers went to who. I didn't find a card."

The two left, whispering together.

Holly smiled as she watched them walk out the front door together.

Trent clasped her hand and escorted her and the boys back to her apartment. Together they tucked her sons into bed. All four of them knelt by the twins' beds while the boys prayed their nightly prayers.

"You need to sleep tight, so you can go to work with me tomorrow. No roughhousing. Go right to sleep." She kissed each boy's cheek.

She and Trent slipped back into the living room.

"Fantastic boys!" Trent grinned and settled on the couch in front of the fire.

She brought two cups of hot cider sprinkled with cinnamon, set the steaming cups on the coffee table, then scrunched on the couch beside him.

After they drank, they placed the boys' Christmas presents under the tree. Trent brought out two he had wrapped for the boys.

Holly clasped her hands and gazed at the star-topped Christmas tree. "Thanks for inviting us. We had a joyful time tonight."

"Let's make it even better." Trent slipped down on one knee on the floor to face her. "Holly Belle Silver, I love you with all my heart. I've loved you since I first saw your face in Calculus Class. You walked into the room wearing your pink turtle-neck sweater and plaid skirt with your long hair curled around your face. I couldn't breathe right. I thought you were a dream-walking. Your still one. I know now that I'll never love anyone else. I'll never leave you again. Will you do me the honor of becoming my life partner?"

"Trent, I too believe in love at first sight. The first date I had with you when I had to sit through that horror movie, *Revenge of the Creature*, and you held my hand, I fell in love with you…and never stopped. The boys love you. I love you. I'm sure being the wife of a detective will be wild, but yes. I'll marry you." She grabbed his hands. "Besides, I still need that portrait of the twins."

Trent laughed from deep within his chest. "We could make that a family portrait." He sprang up and swept her into his arms. He kissed her as if he'd been in the desert way too long and she was life-saving water. When he finished he held her at arm's length and gazed into her eyes. "Sorry I don't have a ring. It's my Christmas present to you, but I want you to choose the one you like."

"Pretty certain, were you?" She kissed him. Then plopped on the couch and drew him with her.

He shook his head. "Nope. But I wasn't about to give you up." He pulled a small box from his pocket. "I bought a back-up present in case you refused."

"May I open it tonight?"

"Sure. We'll shop for your real present tomorrow."

She pulled off the wrapping. "Oh, Trent! It's lovely." She shook her head. "But it must have cost a fortune." She held out her wrist for him to attach the diamond bracelet.

"I didn't want to influence your decision, but I made a killing trading stocks over the past few years. If you want to quit work and stay at home raising the boys…and our other children, we can work that out. Your choice."

"I've always wanted to be a stay-at-home mom."

"I don't want to wait long. Seems to me the ten years I've already waited was way too long." He traced a finger over her lips. "Though you're worth the wait. Let's get the license. We can get married at church on Christmas Day and spend our honeymoon at The Magnolia Manor B & B here in Williamsburg. I have to report for duty in one week."

"Do you think your parents will want to attend?"

"I've been talking to them about you and the boys for days. They wouldn't miss our wedding. They'll hire a private plane if they need to."

"What ever happened to taking things slow?" She melted into his arms.

Chapter 16

Christmas Day 1955

Holly stood at the front of the church waiting her cue. "This Christmas has turned out to be so much more joyous than last Christmas."

Shirley adjusted the cap sleeve to her red taffeta ballerina dress. "You had a rough year last year."

Holly loosened her death lock on her wedding bouquet. "My heart still aches, but I'm no longer devastated. No longer feel I can't face the world alone."

"You don't have to. You have Trent…and me."

Holly nodded. "Mom would have loved helping with the wedding preparations." Holly fluffed her veil over her face. "I still miss Mom's caring touch. Time has eased the pain."

"Yeah. Time's good for something besides putting wrinkles in my face."

Holly laughed. "This year I can picture Mom peering

out a heavenly window and tossing down blessings and good wishes for a long and happy life."

Shirley turned to face the door and stood at attention. "That's my music." Her dress rustled as she departed to glide down the church aisle.

Trent and his best friend, whom Holly had yet to meet, waited beside the altar at the front. Both tall and striking in their white dinner jackets. Each with a red rose in his lapel.

A friend of Shirley's stood in the alcove beside the organ and sang *Always.*

Tears pricked Holly's eyes.

The organ broke out with the Mendelssohn Wedding March.

The redhaired twins, wearing full white tuxes, rushed to her side, one tripping on the white runner that ran down the aisle. Each grabbed one of her hands and walked her down the candlelit aisle. Randy carried her bouquet. Once the boys recognized familiar faces, they strutted like wooden soldiers, huge smiles lighting their freckled faces.

Holly's white ballerina slippers floated down the aisle between them.

She glimpsed friends on both sides of the aisle. Trent's beaming parents reigned in the front row. Holly and Shirley's fellow workers, neighbors, and friends filled the front section of the church.

Poinsettias bloomed everywhere.

The boys dropped her hands, Randy passed her the wedding bouquet, and they scooted into the pew next to

Trent's parents without any mishaps.

Trent welcomed her with a smile that made her heart sing.

Before she knew it, the young pastor pronounced them man and wife.

Tears pricked Holly's eyes as her groom took her into his arms and kissed her as if he would never let her go.

The photographer flashed his camera, popped out bulbs, and flashed again. After pictures of the wedding party and family, they all trooped over to *Ye Olde Queen's Inn* where Charlie presided over a three-tiered wedding cake. He'd opened the doors to the Event Room, so customers could glimpse the wedding reception and sit-down dinner.

The reception was flawless.

Mr. John Baxter approached the wedding table, carrying a plate of bridal cake in one hand and a wedding present in the other. "Best wishes to a fine couple. I'll see you both at parents' conference."

After guests gathered at one end of the long room, Holly tossed her bouquet of white roses over her shoulder to Shirley. Her friend beamed at Seth, who ran a finger around his collar under his tie, but grinned.

Inside the bride's room, Holly changed into a red suit with a white fur collar. After more photographs, she and Trent ran for the silver car trailing cans and old shoes. Someone had scrawled *Just Married* across the back window.

Holly's mouth dropped. "Wow! A BMW. Is it yours?"

"Yep."

A limo stopped at the curb. Mr. and Mrs. Conway motioned for Rake and Randy to join them. Holly had balked at Trent's parents caring for the boys while she and Trent honeymooned. But during the rehearsal dinner, the older couple overcame her concerns and their love burrowed deep into her brimming heart. They'd insisted. She learned they were used to getting their own way. She'd have her work cut out for her standing on her own two feet, but fortunately Trent's parents lived six hundred miles away.

She and Trent ran to the BMW amid a shower of rice. Everyone massed on the sidewalk called "Congratulations!"

She couldn't have asked for a more beautiful or happy wedding.

The BMW slid to the curb in front of an old-fashioned, Federal Style, two-story brick building.

A huge Christmas wreath hung over the door to the Magnolia Manor B & B.

He carried her over the threshold without even breathing hard.

Finally, they faced each other in the bridal suite.

Holly wrapped her arms around her new husband's neck. "I thought I moved to Williamsburg for a few magical months. God had other plans. I fell in love with the village."

"And with me?" Trent's lips nibbled her neck in the tender spot beneath her ear.

She giggled. "Yes, with you. Here, with you by my

side, the magic of Christmas will last all year long."

"You're a Christmas miracle yourself! Shall we make Williamsburg our home?" His warm lips travelled to her cheek and then to the corner of her mouth.

"Isn't this where you work?"

"It is." He kissed her long and thoroughly.

When she came up for air, she pulled in a deep, happy breath. "Then this is home. The boys love it here. And so do I. I can't think of anyplace I'd rather live." She caressed his cheek. "Or anyone I'd rather be married to. I love you truly."

Trent smiled, but his eyes looked dark and serious. "For as long as we both shall live. I'll never leave you."

ANNE GREENE

Dear Reader,

I so hope you enjoyed reading A WILLIAMSBURG CHRISTMAS as much as I loved writing the novella. I've written several other books and novellas. My latest books, LACEY AND THE LAW, TEXAS LAW, A CRAZY OPTIMIST, HER RELUCTANT HERO, and MYSTERY AT DEAD BROKE RANCH all released this year. You might also be interested in reading my other novellas: AVOIDING THE MISTLETOE, A REBEL SPY, LORD BENTLEY NEEDS A BRIDE, KEARA'S ESCAPE, A CHRISTMAS BELLE, THE MARRIAGE BROKER AND THE MORTICIAN, DAREDEVILS, SPUR OF THE MOMENT BRIDE, A GROOM FOR CHRISTMAS, and A TEXAS CHRISTMAS MYSTERY.

I love writing about alpha heroes who aren't afraid to fall on their knees in prayer, and about gutsy heroines. Moody Press published my first book, TRAIL OF TEARS. My *Women of Courage* series spotlights heroic women of World War II. You might want to begin with the first book ANGEL WITH STEEL WINGS. Read my HOLLY GARDEN PRIVATE INVESTIGATOR series. The first book is RED IS FOR

ROOKIE. Enjoy my award-winning Scottish historical romances, MASQUERADE MARRIAGE and MARRIAGE BY ARRANGEMENT. I hope my stories transport you to awesome new worlds and touch your heart to seek a deeper spiritual relationship with the Lord Jesus.

Buy my books on https://www.amazon.com/Anne-Greene/e/B004ECUWMG

I find it a pleasure to speak with my readers. I hope you'll visit with me at www.AnneGreeneAuthor.com and www.facebook.com/AnneWGreeneAuthor. I enjoy discovering what you think about my books and about other Christian books you love.

I'm expecting to hear from you. If you'd like to subscribe to my newsletter, please JOIN MY NEWSLETTER at https://www.AnneGreeneAuthor.com.

Thank you for reading A WILLIAMSBURG CHRISTMAS. Please consider telling your friends or posting a short review on Amazon or Good Reads. Word of mouth is an author's best friend and much appreciated.

ANNE GREENE BIO

My home is in the quaint antiquing town of McKinney, Texas, just a few miles north of Dallas. My dear husband is a retired Colonel, Army Special Forces. My little blonde and white Shih Tzu, Lily Valentine, shares my writing space, curled at my feet. I have four beautiful, talented children, and eight grandchildren who keep me on my toes.

I've lived in or traveled to every location of each book I've written, and each book is a book of my heart. Besides my first love, writing, I enjoy travel, art, reading, movies, and way too many other things to mention. Life is good. Jesus said, "I am come that you might have life and that you might have it more abundantly." Whether writing contemporary or historical, my books celebrate the abundant life Jesus gives.

You will find all my books listed on my website, http://www.AnneGreeneAuthor.com or on Amazon.com.

- Angel with Steel Wings
- Red is for Rookie
- Holly Garden, PI: Red Is for Rookie
- Masquerade Marriage
- Marriage By Arrangement
- A Texas Christmas Mystery
- A Christmas Belle (Christmas Mail Order Angels)
- The California Gold Rush Romance Collection: 9 Stories of Finding Treasures Worth   More than Gold

Keara's Escape (A Spinster Orphan Train novella)
Daredevils
Spur of the Moment Bride
A Groom for Christmas
Avoiding the Mistletoe
A Rebel Spy
Lord Bentley Needs A Bride
Mystery at Dead Broke Ranch
Her Reluctant Hero
A Crazy Optimist
Texas Law
Lacy and the Law

Anne Greene Author Home Page
Anne Greene's Books on Amazon

www.ingramcontent.com/pod-product-compliance
Lightning Source LLC
LaVergne TN
LVHW012026060526
838201LV00061B/4479